THE BOY IN THE STRIPED PYJAMAS

www.**books**at**transworld**.co.uk

THE BOY IN THE STRIPED PYJAMAS

a fable
by
John Boyne

Doubleday

LONDON · TORONTO · SYDNEY · AUCKLAND · JOHANNESBURG

TRANSWORLD PUBLISHERS
61–63 Uxbridge Road, London W5 5SA
a division of The Random House Group Ltd

RANDOM HOUSE AUSTRALIA (PTY) LTD
20 Alfred Street, Milsons Point, Sydney,
New South Wales 2061, Australia

RANDOM HOUSE NEW ZEALAND LTD
18 Poland Road, Glenfield, Auckland 10, New Zealand

RANDOM HOUSE SOUTH AFRICA (PTY) LTD
Isle of Houghton, Corner of Boundary Road & Carse O'Gowrie,
Houghton 2198, South Africa

Published 2006 by Doubleday
a division of Transworld Publishers

A catalogue record for this book is available
from the British Library.
ISBN 9780385611350 (from Jan 07) (cased)
ISBN 0385611358 (cased)
ISBN 9780385611619 (from Jan 07) (tpb)
ISBN 0385611617 (tpb)

Typeset in 12/15pt New Baskerville

Printed and bound in Great Britain by
Clays Ltd, Bungay, Suffolk

1 3 5 7 9 10 8 6 4 2

Papers used by Transworld Publishers are natural, recyclable products
made from wood grown in sustainable forests. The manufacturing processes
conform to the environmental regulations of the country of origin.

For Jamie Lynch

Acknowledgements

For all their advice and insightful comments and for never allowing me to lose my focus on the story, many thanks to David Fickling, Bella Pearson and Linda Sargent. And for getting behind this from the start thanks, as ever, to my agent Simon Trewin.

Thanks also to my old friend Janette Jenkins for her great encouragement after reading an early draft.

Chapter One

Bruno Makes a Discovery

One afternoon, when Bruno came home from school, he was surprised to find Maria, the family's maid – who always kept her head bowed and never looked up from the carpet – standing in his bedroom, pulling all his belongings out of the wardrobe and packing them in four large wooden crates, even the things he'd hidden at the back that belonged to him and were nobody else's business.

'What are you doing?' he asked in as polite a tone as he could muster, for although he wasn't happy to come home and find someone going through his possessions, his mother had always told him that he was to treat Maria respectfully and not just imitate the way Father spoke to her. 'You take your hands off my things.'

Maria shook her head and pointed towards the staircase behind him, where Bruno's mother had just appeared. She was a tall woman with long red hair that she bundled into a sort of net behind her head, and she was twisting her hands together nervously as if there was something she didn't want to have to say or something she didn't want to have to believe.

'Mother,' said Bruno, marching towards her, 'what's going on? Why is Maria going through my things?'

'She's packing them,' explained Mother.

'Packing them?' he asked, running quickly through the events of the previous few days to consider whether he'd been particularly naughty or had used those words out loud that he wasn't allowed to use and was being sent away because of it. He couldn't think of anything though. In fact over the last few days he had behaved in a perfectly decent manner to everyone and couldn't remember causing any chaos at all. 'Why?' he asked then. 'What have I done?'

Mother had walked into her own bedroom by then but Lars, the butler, was in there, packing her things too. She sighed and threw her hands in the air in frustration before marching back to the staircase, followed by Bruno, who wasn't going to let the matter drop without an explanation.

'Mother,' he insisted. 'What's going on? Are we moving?'

'Come downstairs with me,' said Mother, leading the way towards the large dining room where the Fury had been to dinner the week before. 'We'll talk down there.'

Bruno ran downstairs and even passed her out on the staircase so that he was waiting in the dining room when she arrived. He looked at her without saying anything for a moment and thought to himself that she couldn't have applied her make-up correctly that morning because the rims of her eyes were more red than usual, like his own after he'd been causing chaos and got into trouble and ended up crying.

'Now, you don't have to worry, Bruno,' said Mother, sitting down in the chair where the beautiful blonde woman who had come to dinner with the Fury had sat and waved at him when Father closed the doors. 'In fact if anything it's going to be a great adventure.'

'What is?' he asked. 'Am I being sent away?'

'No, not just you,' she said, looking as if she might smile for a moment but thinking better of it. 'We all are. Your father and I, Gretel and you. All four of us.'

Bruno thought about this and frowned. He wasn't particularly bothered if Gretel was being sent away because she was a Hopeless Case and caused nothing but trouble for him. But it seemed a little unfair that they all had to go with her.

'But where?' he asked. 'Where are we going exactly? Why can't we stay here?'

'Your father's job,' explained Mother. 'You know how important it is, don't you?'

'Yes, of course,' said Bruno, nodding his head, because there were always so many visitors to the house – men in fantastic uniforms, women with type-writers that he had to keep his mucky hands off – and they were always very polite to Father and told each other that he was a man to watch and that the Fury had big things in mind for him.

'Well, sometimes when someone is very important,' continued Mother, 'the man who employs him asks him to go somewhere else because there's a very special job that needs doing there.'

'What kind of job?' asked Bruno, because if he was honest with himself – which he always tried to be – he wasn't entirely sure what job Father did.

In school they had talked about their fathers one day and Karl had said that his father was a green-grocer, which Bruno knew to be true because he ran the greengrocer's shop in the centre of town. And Daniel had said that his father was a teacher, which Bruno knew to be true because he taught the big boys who it was always wise to steer clear of. And Martin had said that his father was a chef, which Bruno knew to be true because he sometimes collected Martin from school and when he did he always wore a white smock and a tartan apron, as if he'd just stepped out of his kitchen.

But when they asked Bruno what his father did he opened his mouth to tell them, then realized that he didn't know himself. All he could say was that his father was a man to watch and that the Fury had big things in mind for him. Oh, and that he had a fantastic uniform too.

'It's a very important job,' said Mother, hesitating for a moment. 'A job that needs a very special man to do it. You can understand that, can't you?'

'And we all have to go too?' asked Bruno.

'Of course we do,' said Mother. 'You wouldn't want Father to go to his new job on his own and be lonely there, would you?'

'I suppose not,' said Bruno.

'Father would miss us all terribly if we weren't with him,' she added.

'Who would he miss the most?' asked Bruno. 'Me or Gretel?'

'He would miss you both equally,' said Mother, for she was a great believer in not playing favourites, which Bruno respected, especially since he knew that he was her favourite really.

'But what about our house?' asked Bruno. 'Who's going to take care of it while we're gone?'

Mother sighed and looked around the room as if she might never see it again. It was a very beautiful house and had five floors in total, if you included the basement, where Cook made all the food and Maria and Lars sat at the table arguing with each other and calling each other names that you weren't supposed to use. And if you added in the little room at the top of the house with the slanted windows where Bruno could see right across Berlin if he stood up on his tiptoes and held onto the frame tightly.

'We have to close up the house for now,' said Mother. 'But we'll come back to it someday.'

'And what about Cook?' asked Bruno. 'And Lars? And Maria? Are they not going to live in it?'

'They're coming with us,' explained Mother. 'But that's enough questions for now. Maybe you should go upstairs and help Maria with your packing.'

Bruno stood up from the seat but didn't go anywhere. There were just a few more questions he needed to put to her before he could allow the matter to be settled.

'And how far away is it?' he asked. 'The new job, I mean. Is it further than a mile away?'

'Oh my,' said Mother with a laugh, although it was a strange kind of laugh because she didn't look happy and turned away from Bruno as if she didn't want him to see her face. 'Yes, Bruno,' she said. 'It's more than a mile away. Quite a lot more than that, in fact.'

Bruno's eyes opened wide and his mouth made the shape of an O. He felt his arms stretching out at his sides like they did whenever something surprised him. 'You don't mean we're leaving Berlin?' he asked, gasping for air as he got the words out.

'I'm afraid so,' said Mother, nodding her head sadly. 'Your father's job is—'

'But what about school?' said Bruno, interrupting her, a thing he knew he was not supposed to do but which he felt he would be forgiven for on this occasion. 'And what about Karl and Daniel and Martin? How will they know where I am when we want to do things together?'

'You'll have to say goodbye to your friends for the time being,' said Mother. 'Although I'm sure you'll see them again in time. And don't interrupt your mother when she's talking, please,' she added, for although this was strange and unpleasant news, there was certainly no need for Bruno to break the rules of politeness which he had been taught.

'Say goodbye to them?' he asked, staring at her in surprise. 'Say goodbye to them?' he repeated, spluttering out the words as if his mouth was full of biscuits that he'd munched into tiny pieces but not actually swallowed yet. 'Say goodbye to Karl and Daniel and Martin?' he continued, his voice coming dangerously close to shouting, which was not allowed indoors. 'But they're my three best friends for life!'

'Oh, you'll make other friends,' said Mother, waving her hand in the air dismissively, as if the making of a boy's three best friends for life was an easy thing.

'But we had plans,' he protested.

'Plans?' asked Mother, raising an eyebrow. 'What sort of plans?'

'Well, that would be telling,' said Bruno, who could not reveal the exact nature of the plans – which included causing a lot of chaos, especially in a few weeks' time when school finished for the summer holidays and they didn't have to spend all their time just making plans but could actually put them into effect instead.

'I'm sorry, Bruno,' said Mother, 'but your plans are just going to have to wait. We don't have a choice in this.'

'But, Mother!'

'Bruno, that's enough,' she said, snapping at him now and standing up to show him that she was serious when she said that was enough. 'Honestly, only last week you were complaining about how much things have changed here recently.'

'Well, I don't like the way we have to turn all the lights off at night now,' he admitted.

'Everyone has to do that,' said Mother. 'It keeps us safe. And who knows, maybe we'll be in less danger if we move away. Now, I need you to go upstairs and help Maria with your packing. We don't have as much time to prepare as I would have liked, thanks to some people.'

Bruno nodded and walked away sadly, knowing

that 'some people' was a grown-up's word for 'Father' and one that he wasn't supposed to use himself.

He made his way up the stairs slowly, holding onto the banister with one hand, and wondered whether the new house in the new place where the new job was would have as fine a banister to slide down as this one did. For the banister in this house stretched from the very top floor – just outside the little room where, if he stood on his tiptoes and held onto the frame of the window tightly, he could see right across Berlin – to the ground floor, just in front of the two enormous oak doors. And Bruno liked nothing better than to get on board the banister at the top floor and slide his way through the house, making whooshing sounds as he went.

Down from the top floor to the next one, where Mother and Father's room was, and the large bath-room, and where he wasn't supposed to be in any case.

Down to the next floor, where his own room was, and Gretel's room too, and the smaller bathroom which he was supposed to use more often than he really did.

Down to the ground floor, where you fell off the end of the banister and had to land flat on your two feet or it was five points against you and you had to start all over again.

The banister was the best thing about this house –
that and the fact that Grandfather and Grandmother
lived so near by – and when he thought about that it
made him wonder whether they were coming to the
new job too and he presumed that they were because
they could hardly be left behind. No one needed
Gretel much because she was a Hopeless Case – it
would be a lot easier if she stayed to look after the
house – but Grandfather and Grandmother? Well,
that was an entirely different matter.

Bruno went up the stairs slowly towards his room,
but before going inside he looked back down
towards the ground floor and saw Mother entering
Father's office, which faced the dining room – and
was Out Of Bounds At All Times And No
Exceptions – and he heard her speaking loudly to
him until Father spoke louder than Mother could
and that put a stop to their conversation. Then the
door of the office closed and Bruno couldn't hear any
more so he thought it would be a good idea if he
went back to his room and took over the packing
from Maria, because otherwise she might pull all his
belongings out of the wardrobe without any care or
consideration, even the things he'd hidden at the
back that belonged to him and were nobody else's
business.

Chapter Two

The New House

When he first saw their new house Bruno's eyes opened wide, his mouth made the shape of an O and his arms stretched out at his sides once again. Everything about it seemed to be the exact opposite of their old home and he couldn't believe that they were really going to live there.

The house in Berlin had stood on a quiet street and alongside it were a handful of other big houses like his own, and it was always nice to look at them because they were almost the same as his house but not quite, and other boys lived in them who he played with (if they were friends) or steered clear of (if they were trouble). The new house, however, stood all on its own in an empty, desolate place and there were no other houses anywhere to be seen, which meant there would be no other families around and no other boys to play with, neither friends nor trouble.

The house in Berlin was enormous, and even

though he'd lived there for nine years he was still able to find nooks and crannies that he hadn't fully finished exploring yet. There were even whole rooms – such as Father's office, which was Out Of Bounds At All Times And No Exceptions – that he had barely been inside. However, the new house had only three floors: a top floor where all three bedrooms were and only one bathroom, a ground floor with a kitchen, a dining room and a new office for Father (which, he presumed, had the same restrictions as the old one), and a basement where the servants slept.

All around the house in Berlin were other streets of large houses, and when you walked towards the centre of town there were always people strolling along and stopping to chat to each other or rushing around and saying they had no time to stop, not today, not when they had a hundred and one things to do. There were shops with bright store fronts, and fruit and vegetable stalls with big trays piled high with cabbages, carrots, cauliflowers and corn. Some were overspilling with leeks and mushrooms, turnips and sprouts; others with lettuce and green beans, courgettes and parsnips. Sometimes he liked to stand in front of these stalls and close his eyes and breathe in their aromas, feeling his head grow dizzy with the mixed scents of sweetness and life. But there were no other streets around the new house, no one strolling along or rushing around, and definitely no shops or fruit and vegetable stalls. When he closed his eyes, everything around him just felt empty and cold, as if he was in the loneliest place in the world. The middle of nowhere.

In Berlin there had been tables set out on the street, and sometimes when he walked home from school with Karl, Daniel and Martin there would be men and women sitting at them, drinking frothy drinks and laughing loudly; the people who sat at these tables must be very funny people, he always thought, because it didn't matter what they said, somebody always laughed. But there was something about the new house that made Bruno think that no one ever laughed there; that there was nothing to laugh at and nothing to be happy about.

'I think this was a bad idea,' said Bruno a few hours after they arrived, while Maria was unpacking his suitcases upstairs. (Maria wasn't the only maid at the new house either: there were three others who were quite skinny and only ever spoke to each other in whispering voices. There was an old man too who, he was told, was there to prepare the vegetables every day and wait on them at the dinner table, and who looked very unhappy but also a little angry.)

'We don't have the luxury of thinking,' said Mother, opening a box that contained the set of sixty-four glasses that Grandfather and Grandmother

13

had given her when she married Father. 'Some people make all the decisions for us.'

Bruno didn't know what she meant by that so he pretended that she'd never said it at all. 'I think this was a bad idea,' he repeated. 'I think the best thing to do would be to forget all about this and just go back home. We can chalk it up to experience,' he added, a phrase he had learned recently and was determined to use as often as possible.

Mother smiled and put the glasses down carefully on the table. 'I have another phrase for you,' she said. 'It's that we have to make the best of a bad situation.'

'Well, I don't know that we do,' said Bruno. 'I think you should just tell Father that you've changed your mind and, well, if we have to stay here for the rest of the day and have dinner here this evening and sleep here tonight because we're all tired, then that's all right, but we should probably get up early in the morning if we're to make it back to Berlin by tea-time tomorrow.'

Mother sighed. 'Bruno, why don't you just go upstairs and help Maria unpack?' she asked.

'But there's no point unpacking if we're only going to—'

'Bruno, just do it, please!' snapped Mother, because apparently it was all right if she interrupted him but it didn't work the other way round. 'We're here, we've arrived, this is our home for the foreseeable future and we just have to make the best of things. Do you understand me?'

He didn't understand what the 'foreseeable future' meant and told her so.

'It means that this is where we live now, Bruno,' said Mother. 'And that's an end to it.'

Bruno had a pain in his stomach and he could feel something growing inside him, something that when it worked its way up from the lowest depths inside him to the outside world would either make him shout and scream that the whole thing was wrong and unfair and a big mistake for which somebody would pay one of these days, or just make him burst into tears instead. He couldn't understand how this had all come about. One day he was perfectly content, playing at home, having three best friends for life, sliding down banisters, trying to stand on his tiptoes to see right across Berlin, and now he was stuck here in this cold, nasty house with three whispering maids and a waiter who was both unhappy and angry, where no one looked as if they could ever be cheerful again.

'Bruno, I want you to go upstairs and unpack and I want you to do it now,' said Mother in an unfriendly voice, and he knew that she meant business so he turned round and marched away without another word. He could feel tears springing up behind his eyes but he was determined that he wouldn't allow them to appear.

He went upstairs and turned slowly around in a full circle, hoping he might find a small door or cubby hole where a decent amount of exploration could eventually be done, but there wasn't one. On his floor there were just four doors, two on either side, facing each other. A door into his room, a door into Gretel's room, a door into Mother and Father's room, and a door into the bathroom.

'This isn't home and it never will be,' he muttered under his breath as he went through his own door to find all his clothes scattered on the bed and the boxes of toys and books not even unpacked yet. It was obvious that Maria did not have her priorities right.

'Mother sent me to help,' he said quietly, and Maria nodded and pointed towards a big bag that contained all his socks and vests and underpants.

'If you sort that lot out, you could put them in the chest of drawers over there,' she said, pointing towards an ugly chest that stood across the room beside a mirror that was covered in dust.

Bruno sighed and opened the bag; it was full to the brim with his underwear and he wanted nothing more than to crawl inside it and hope that when he climbed out again he'd have woken up and be back home again.

'What do you think of all this, Maria?' he asked

after a long silence because he had always liked Maria and felt as if she was one of the family, even though Father said she was just a maid and overpaid at that.

'All what?' she asked.

'This,' he said as if it was the most obvious thing in the world. 'Coming to a place like this. Don't you think we've made a big mistake?'

'That's not for me to say, Master Bruno,' said Maria. 'Your mother has explained to you about your father's job and—'

'Oh, I'm tired of hearing about Father's job,' said Bruno, interrupting her. 'That's all we ever hear about, if you ask me. Father's job this and Father's job that. Well, if Father's job means that we have to move away from our house and the sliding banister and my three best friends for life, then I think Father should think twice about his job, don't you?'

Just at that moment there was a creak outside in the hallway and Bruno looked up to see the door of Mother and Father's room opening slightly. He froze, unable to move for a moment. Mother was still downstairs, which meant that Father was in there and he might have heard everything that Bruno had just said. He watched the door, hardly daring to breathe, wondering whether Father might come through it and take him downstairs for a serious talking-to.

The door opened wider and Bruno stepped back

as a figure appeared, but it wasn't Father. It was a much younger man, and not as tall as Father either, but he wore the same type of uniform, only without as many decorations on it. He looked very serious and his cap was secured tightly on his head. Around his temples Bruno could see that he had very blond hair, an almost unnatural shade of yellow. He was carrying a box in his hands and walking towards the staircase, but he stopped for a moment when he saw Bruno standing there watching him. He looked the boy up and down as if he had never seen a child before and wasn't quite sure what he was supposed to do with one: eat it, ignore it or kick it down the stairs. Instead he gave Bruno a quick nod and continued on his way.

'Who was that?' asked Bruno. The young man had seemed so serious and busy that he assumed he must be someone very important.

'One of your father's soldiers, I suppose,' said Maria, who had stood up very straight when the young man appeared and held her hands before her like a person in prayer. She had stared down at the ground rather than at his face, as if she was afraid she might be turned to stone if she looked directly at him; she only relaxed when he had gone. 'We'll get to know them in time.'

'I don't think I like him,' said Bruno. 'He was too serious.'

'Your father is very serious too,' said Maria.

'Yes, but he's Father,' explained Bruno. 'Fathers are supposed to be serious. It doesn't matter whether they're greengrocers or teachers or chefs or commandants,' he said, listing all the jobs that he knew decent, respectable fathers did and whose titles he had thought about a thousand times. 'And I don't think that man looked like a father. Although he was very serious, that's for sure.'

'Well, they have very serious jobs,' said Maria with a sigh. 'Or so they think anyway. But if I was you I'd steer clear of the soldiers.'

'I don't see what else there is to do other than that,' said Bruno sadly. 'I don't even think there's going to be anyone to play with other than Gretel, and what fun is that after all? She's a Hopeless Case.'

He felt as if he was about to cry again but stopped himself, not wanting to look like a baby in front of Maria. He looked around the room without fully lifting his eyes up from the ground, trying to see whether there was anything of interest to be found. There wasn't. Or there didn't seem to be. But then one thing caught his eye. Over in the corner of the room opposite the door there was a window in the ceiling that stretched down into the wall, a little like the one on the top floor of the house in Berlin, only not so high. Bruno looked at it and thought that he might be able to see out without even having to stand on tiptoes.

He walked slowly towards it, hoping that from here he might be able to see all the way back to Berlin and his house and the streets around it and the tables where the people sat and drank their frothy drinks and told each other hilarious stories. He walked slowly because he didn't want to be disappointed. But it was just a small boy's room and there was only so far he could walk before he arrived at the window. He put his face to the glass and saw what was out there, and this time when his eyes opened wide and his mouth made the shape of an O, his hands stayed by his sides because something made him feel very cold and unsafe.

Chapter Three

The Hopeless Case

Bruno was sure that it would have made a lot more sense if they had left Gretel behind in Berlin to look after the house because she was nothing but trouble. In fact he had heard her described on any number of occasions as being Trouble From Day One.

Gretel was three years older than Bruno and she had made it clear to him from as far back as he could remember that when it came to the ways of the world, particularly any events within that world that concerned the two of them, she was in charge. Bruno didn't like to admit that he was a little scared of her, but if he was honest with himself – which he always tried to be – he would have admitted that he was.

She had some nasty habits, as was to be expected from sisters. She spent far too long in the bathroom in the mornings for one thing, and didn't seem to mind if Bruno was left outside, hopping from foot to foot, desperate to go.

She had a large collection of dolls positioned on

shelves around her room that stared at Bruno when he went inside and followed him around, watching whatever he did. He was sure that if he went exploring in her room when she was out of the house, they would report back to her on everything he did. She had some very unpleasant friends too, who seemed to think that it was clever to make fun of him, a thing he never would have done if he had been three years older than her. All Gretel's unpleasant friends seemed to enjoy nothing more than torturing him and said nasty things to him whenever Mother or Maria were nowhere in sight.

'Bruno's not nine, he's only six,' said one particular monster over and over again in a sing-song voice, dancing around him and poking him in the ribs.

'I'm not six, I'm nine,' he protested, trying to get away.

'Then why are you so small?' asked the monster. 'All the other nine-year-olds are bigger than you.'

This was true, and a particular sore point for Bruno. It was a source of constant disappointment to him that he wasn't as tall as any of the other boys in his class. In fact he only came up to their shoulders. Whenever he walked along the streets with Karl, Daniel and Martin, people sometimes mistook him for the younger brother of one of them when in fact he was the second oldest.

'So you must be only six,' insisted the monster, and Bruno would run away and do his stretching exercises and hope that he would wake up one morning and have grown an extra foot or two.

So one good thing about not being in Berlin any more was the fact that none of them would be around to torture him. Perhaps if he was forced to stay at the new house for a while, even as long as a month, he would have grown by the time they returned home and then they wouldn't be able to be mean to him any more. It was something to keep in mind anyway if he wanted to do what Mother had suggested and make the best of a bad situation.

He ran into Gretel's room without knocking and discovered her placing her civilization of dolls on various shelves around the room.

'What are you doing in here?' she shouted, spinning round. 'Don't you know you don't enter a lady's room without knocking?'

'You didn't bring all your dolls with you, surely?' asked Bruno, who had developed a habit of ignoring most of his sister's questions and asking a few of his own in their place.

'Of course I did,' she replied. 'You don't think I'd have left them at home? Why, it could be weeks before we're back there again.'

'Weeks?' said Bruno, sounding disappointed but

secretly pleased because he'd resigned himself to the idea of spending a month there. 'Do you really think so?'

'Well, I asked Father and he said we would be here for the foreseeable future.'

'What is the foreseeable future exactly?' asked Bruno, sitting down on the side of her bed.

'It means weeks from now,' said Gretel with an intelligent nod of her head. 'Perhaps as long as three.'

'That's all right then,' said Bruno. 'As long as it's just for the foreseeable future and not for a month. I hate it here.'

Gretel looked at her little brother and found herself agreeing with him for once. 'I know what you mean,' she said. 'It's not very nice, is it?'

'It's horrible,' said Bruno.

'Well, yes,' said Gretel, acknowledging that. 'It's horrible right now. But once the house is smartened up a bit it probably won't seem so bad. I heard Father say that whoever lived here at Out-With before us lost their job very quickly and didn't have time to make the place nice for us.'

'Out-With?' asked Bruno. 'What's an Out-With?'

'It's not *an* Out-With, Bruno,' said Gretel with a sigh. 'It's just Out-With.'

'Well, what's Out-With then?' he repeated. 'Out with what?'

'That's the name of the house,' explained Gretel. 'Out-With.'

Bruno considered this. He hadn't seen any sign on the outside to say that was what it was called, nor had he seen any writing on the front door. His own house back in Berlin didn't even have a name; it was just called number four.

'But what does it mean?' he asked in exasperation. 'Out with what?'

'Out with the people who lived here before us, I expect,' said Gretel. 'It must have to do with the fact that he didn't do a very good job and someone said out with him and let's get a man in who can do it right.'

'You mean Father.'

'Of course,' said Gretel, who always spoke of Father as if he could never do any wrong and never got angry and always came in to kiss her goodnight before she went to sleep which, if Bruno was to be really fair and not just sad about moving houses, he would have admitted Father did for him too.

'So we're here at Out-With because someone said out with the people before us?'

'Exactly, Bruno,' said Gretel. 'Now get off my bedspread. You're messing it up.'

Bruno jumped off the bed and landed with a thud on the carpet. He didn't like the sound it made. It was very hollow and he immediately decided he'd better not go jumping around this house too often or it might collapse around their ears.

'I don't like it here,' he said for the hundredth time.

'I know you don't,' said Gretel. 'But there's nothing we can do about it, is there?'

'I miss Karl and Daniel and Martin,' said Bruno.

'And I miss Hilda and Isobel and Louise,' said Gretel, and Bruno tried to remember which of those three girls was the monster.

'I don't think the other children look at all friendly,' said Bruno, and Gretel immediately stopped putting one of her more terrifying dolls on a shelf and turned round to stare at him.

'What did you just say?' she asked.

'I said I don't think the other children look at all friendly,' he repeated.

'The other children?' said Gretel, sounding confused. 'What other children? I haven't seen any other children.'

Bruno looked around the room. There was a window here but Gretel's room was on the opposite side of the hall, facing his, and so looked in a totally different direction. Trying not to appear too obvious, he strolled casually towards it. He placed his hands in the pockets of his short trousers and attempted to whistle a song he knew while not looking at his sister at all.

'Bruno?' asked Gretel. 'What on earth are you doing? Have you gone mad?'

He continued to stroll and whistle and he continued not to look until he reached the window, which, by a stroke of luck, was also low enough for him to be able to see out of. He looked outside and saw the car they had arrived in, as well as three or four others belonging to the soldiers who worked for Father, some of whom were standing around smoking cigarettes and laughing about something while looking nervously up at the house. Beyond that was the driveway and further along a forest which seemed ripe for exploration.

'Bruno, will you please explain to me what you meant by that last remark?' asked Gretel.

'There's a forest over there,' said Bruno, ignoring her.

'Bruno!' snapped Gretel, marching towards him so quickly that he jumped back from the window and backed up against a wall.

'What?' he asked, pretending not to know what she was talking about.

'The other children,' said Gretel. 'You said they don't look at all friendly.'

'Well, they don't,' said Bruno, not wishing to judge them before he met them but going by appearances, which Mother had told him time and time again not to do.

'But *what* other children?' asked Gretel. 'Where are they?'

Bruno smiled and walked towards the door, indicating that Gretel should follow him. She gave out a deep sigh as she did so, stopping to put the doll on the bed but then changing her mind and picking it up and holding it close to her chest as she went into her brother's room, where she was nearly knocked over by Maria storming out of it holding something that closely resembled a dead mouse.

'They're out there,' said Bruno, who had walked over to his own window again and was looking out of it. He didn't turn back to check that Gretel was in the room; he was too busy watching the children. For a few moments he forgot that she was even there.

Gretel was still a few feet away and desperately wanted to look for herself, but something about the way he had said it and something about the way he was watching made her feel suddenly nervous. Bruno had never been able to trick her before about anything and she was fairly sure that he wasn't tricking her now, but there was something about the way he stood there that made her feel as if she wasn't sure she wanted to see these children at all. She swallowed nervously and said a silent prayer that they would indeed be returning to Berlin in the foreseeable future and not in a month as Bruno had suggested.

'Well?' he said, turning round now and seeing his sister standing in the doorway, clutching the doll, her golden pigtails perfectly balanced on each shoulder, ripe for the pulling. 'Don't you want to see them?'

'Of course I do,' she replied and walked hesitantly towards him. 'Step out of the way then,' she said, elbowing him aside.

It was a bright, sunny day that first afternoon at Out-With and the sun reappeared from behind a cloud just as Gretel looked through the window, but after a moment her eyes adjusted and the sun disappeared again and she saw exactly what Bruno had been talking about.

Chapter Four

What They Saw Through the Window

To begin with, they weren't children at all. Not all of them, at least. There were small boys and big boys, fathers and grandfathers. Perhaps a few uncles too. And some of those people who live on their own on everybody's road but don't seem to have any relatives at all. They were everyone.

'Who are they?' asked Gretel, as open-mouthed as her brother often was these days. 'What sort of place is this?'

'I'm not sure,' said Bruno, sticking as close to the truth as possible. 'But it's not as nice as home, I do know that much.'

'And where are all the girls?' she asked. 'And the mothers? And the grandmothers?'

'Perhaps they live in a different part,' suggested Bruno.

Gretel agreed. She didn't want to go on staring but it was very difficult to turn her eyes away. So far, all she had seen was the forest facing her own window, which looked a little dark but a good place for picnics if there was any sort of clearing further along it. But from this side of the house the view was very different.

It started off nicely enough. There was a garden directly beneath Bruno's window. Quite a large one too, and full of flowers which grew in neat orderly sections in soil that looked as if it was tended very carefully by someone who knew that growing flowers in a place like this was something good that they could do, like putting a tiny candle of light in the corner of a huge castle on a misty moor on a dark winter's night.

Past the flowers there was a very pleasant pavement with a wooden bench on it, where Gretel could imagine sitting in the sunshine and reading a book. There was a plaque attached to the top of the bench but she couldn't read the inscription from this distance. The seat was turned to face the house – which, usually, would be a strange thing to do but on this occasion she could understand why.

About twenty feet further along from the garden and the flowers and the bench with the plaque on it, everything changed. There was a huge wire fence that ran along the length of the house and turned in at the top, extending further along in either direction, further than she could possibly see. The fence was very high, higher even than the house they were standing in, and there were huge wooden posts, like telegraph poles, dotted along it, holding it up. At the top of the fence enormous bales of barbed wire were tangled in spirals, and Gretel felt an unexpected pain inside her as she looked at the sharp spikes sticking out all the way round it.

There wasn't any grass after the fence; in fact there was no greenery anywhere to be seen in the distance. Instead the ground was made of a sand-like substance, and as far as she could make out there was nothing but low huts and large square buildings dotted around and one or two smoke stacks in the distance. She opened her mouth to say something, but when she did she realized that she couldn't find any words to express her surprise, and so she did the only sensible thing she could think of and closed it again.

'You see?' said Bruno from the corner of the room, feeling quietly pleased with himself because whatever it was that was out there – and whoever *they* were – he had seen it first and he could see it whenever he wanted because they were outside his bedroom window and not hers and therefore they belonged to him and he was the king of everything they surveyed and she was his lowly subject.

'I don't understand,' said Gretel. 'Who would build such a nasty-looking place?'

'It *is* a nasty-looking place, isn't it?' agreed Bruno.

'I think those huts have only one floor too. Look how low they are.'

'They must be modern types of houses,' said Gretel. 'Father hates modern things.'

'Then he won't like them very much,' said Bruno.

'No,' replied Gretel. She stood still for a long time staring at them. She was twelve years old and was considered to be one of the brightest girls in her class, so she squeezed her lips together and narrowed her eyes and forced her brain to understand what she was looking at. Finally she could think of only one explanation.

'This must be the countryside,' said Gretel, turning round to look at her brother triumphantly.

'The countryside?'

'Yes, it's the only explanation, don't you see? When we're at home, in Berlin, we're in the city. That's why there are so many people and so many houses and the schools are full and you can't make your way through the centre of town on a Saturday afternoon without getting pushed from pillar to post.'

'Yes . . .' said Bruno, nodding his head, trying to keep up.

'But we learned in geography class that in the countryside, where all the farmers are and the animals, and they grow all the food, there are huge areas like this where people live and work and send all the food to feed us.' She looked out of the window again at the huge area spread out before her and the distances that existed between each of the huts. 'This must be it. It's the countryside. Perhaps this is our holiday home,' she added hopefully.

Bruno thought about it and shook his head. 'I don't think so,' he said with great conviction.

'You're *nine*,' countered Gretel. 'How would you know? When you get to my age you'll understand these things a lot better.'

'That might be so,' said Bruno, who knew that he was younger but didn't agree that that made him less likely to be right, 'but if this is the countryside like you say it is, then where are all the animals you're talking about?'

Gretel opened her mouth to answer him but couldn't think of a suitable reply, so she looked out of the window again instead and peered around for them, but they were nowhere to be seen.

'There should be cows and pigs and sheep and horses,' said Bruno. 'If it was a farm, I mean. Not to mention chickens and ducks.'

'And there aren't any,' admitted Gretel quietly.

'And if they grew food here, like you suggested,' continued Bruno, enjoying himself enormously, 'then I think the ground would have to look a lot better than that, don't you? I don't think you could grow anything in all that dirt.'

Gretel looked at it again and nodded, because she was not so silly as to insist on being in the right all the time when it was clear the argument stood against her.

'Perhaps it's not a farm then,' she said.

'It's not,' agreed Bruno.

'Which means this mightn't be the countryside,' she continued.

'No, I don't think it is,' he replied.

'Which also means that this probably isn't our holiday home after all,' she concluded.

'I don't think so,' said Bruno.

He sat down on the bed and for a moment wished that Gretel would sit down beside him and put her arm around him and tell him that it was all going to be all right and that sooner or later they'd get to like it here and they'd never want to go back to Berlin. But she was still watching from the window and this time she wasn't looking at the flowers or the pavement or the bench with the plaque on it or the tall fence or the wooden telegraph poles or the barbed wire bales or the hard ground beyond them or the huts or the small buildings or the smoke stacks; instead she was looking at the people.

'Who are all those people?' she asked in a quiet voice, almost as if she wasn't asking Bruno but looking for an answer from someone else. 'And what are they all doing there?'

Bruno stood up, and for the first time they stood there together, shoulder to shoulder, and stared at what was happening not fifty feet away from their new home.

Everywhere they looked they could see people, tall, short, old, young, all moving around. Some stood perfectly still in groups, their hands by their sides, trying to keep their heads up, as a soldier marched in front of them, his mouth opening and closing quickly as if he were shouting something at them. Some were formed into a sort of chain gang and pushing wheelbarrows from one side of the camp to the other, appearing from a place out of sight and taking their wheelbarrows further along behind a hut, where they disappeared again. A few stood near the huts in quiet groups, staring at the ground as if it was the sort of game where they didn't want to be spotted. Others were on crutches and many had bandages around their heads. Some carried spades and were being led by groups of soldiers to a place where they could no longer be seen.

Bruno and Gretel could see hundreds of people, but there were so many huts before them, and the camp spread out so much further than they could possibly see, that it looked as though there must be thousands out there.

'And all living so close to us,' said Gretel, frowning.

'In Berlin, on our nice quiet street, we only had six houses. And now there are so many. Why would Father take a new job here in such a nasty place and with so many neighbours? It doesn't make any sense.'

'Look over there,' said Bruno, and Gretel followed the direction of the finger he was pointing and saw, emerging from a hut in the distance, a group of children huddled together and being shouted at by a group of soldiers. The more they were shouted at, the closer they huddled together, but then one of the soldiers lunged towards them and they separated and seemed to do what he had wanted them to do all along, which was to stand in a single line. When they did, the soldiers all started to laugh and applaud them.

'It must be some sort of rehearsal,' suggested Gretel, ignoring the fact that some of the children, even some of the older ones, even the ones as grown up as her, looked as if they were crying.

'I told you there were children here,' said Bruno.

'Not the type of children *I* want to play with,' said Gretel in a determined voice. 'They look filthy. Hilda and Isobel and Louise have a bath every morning and so do I. Those children look like they've never had a bath in their lives.'

'It does look very dirty over there,' said Bruno. 'But maybe they don't have any baths?'

'Don't be stupid,' said Gretel, despite the fact that she had been told time and time again that she was not to call her brother stupid. 'What kind of people don't have baths?'

'I don't know,' said Bruno. 'People who don't have any hot water?'

Gretel watched for another few moments before shivering and turning away. 'I'm going back to my room to arrange my dolls,' she said. 'The view is decidedly nicer from there.'

With that remark she walked away, returning across the hallway to her bedroom and closing the door behind her, but she didn't go back to arranging her dolls quite yet. Instead she sat down on the bed and a lot of things went through her head.

And one final thought came into her brother's head as he watched the hundreds of people in the distance going about their business, and that was the fact that all of them – the small boys, the big boys, the fathers, the grandfathers, the uncles, the people who lived on their own on everybody's road but didn't seem to have any relatives at all – were wearing the same clothes as each other: a pair of grey striped pyjamas with a grey striped cap on their heads.

'How extraordinary,' he muttered, before turning away.

Chapter Five

Out Of Bounds At All Times And No Exceptions

There was only one thing for it and that was to speak to Father.

Father hadn't left Berlin in the car with them that morning. Instead he had left a few days earlier, on the night of the day that Bruno had come home to find Maria going through his things, even the things he'd hidden at the back that belonged to him and were nobody else's business. In the days following, Mother, Gretel, Maria, Cook, Lars and Bruno had spent all their time boxing up their belongings and loading them into a big truck to be brought to their new home at Out-With.

It was on this final morning, when the house looked empty and not like their real home at all, that the very last things they owned were put into suitcases and an official car with red-and-black flags on the front had stopped at their door to take them away.

Mother, Maria and Bruno were the last people to

leave the house and it was Bruno's belief that Mother didn't realize the maid was still standing there, because as they took one last look around the empty hallway where they had spent so many happy times, the place where the Christmas tree stood in December, the place where the wet umbrellas were left in a stand during the winter months, the place where Bruno was supposed to leave his muddy shoes when he came in but never did, Mother had shaken her head and said something very strange.

'We should never have let the Fury come to dinner,' she said. 'Some people and their determination to get ahead.'

Just after she said that she turned round and Bruno could see that she had tears in her eyes, but she jumped when she saw Maria standing there, watching her.

'Maria,' she said, in a startled tone of voice. 'I thought you were in the car.'

'I was just leaving, ma'am,' said Maria.

'I didn't mean—' began Mother before shaking her head and starting again. 'I wasn't trying to suggest—'

'I was just leaving, ma'am,' repeated Maria, who must not have known the rule about not interrupting Mother, and stepped through the door quickly and ran to the car.

Mother had frowned but then shrugged, as if none

of it really mattered any more anyway. 'Come on then, Bruno,' she said, taking his hand and locking the door behind them. 'Let's just hope we get to come back here someday when all this is over.'

The official car with the flags on the front had taken them to a train station, where there were two tracks separated by a wide platform, and on either side a train stood waiting for the passengers to board. Because there were so many soldiers marching about on the other side, not to mention the fact that there was a long hut belonging to the signalman separating the tracks, Bruno could only make out the crowds of people for a few moments before he and his family boarded a very comfortable train with very few people on it and plenty of empty seats and fresh air when the windows were pulled down. If the trains had been going in different directions, he thought, it wouldn't have seemed so odd, but they weren't; they were both pointed eastwards. For a moment he considered running across the platform to tell the people about the empty seats in his carriage, but he decided not to as something told him that if it didn't make Mother angry, it would probably make Gretel furious, and that would be worse still.

Since arriving at Out-With and their new house, Bruno hadn't seen his father. He had thought perhaps he was in his bedroom earlier when the door creaked open, but that had turned out to be the unfriendly young soldier who had stared at Bruno without any warmth in his eyes. He hadn't heard Father's booming voice anywhere and he hadn't heard the heavy sound of his boots on the floor-boards downstairs. But there were definitely people coming and going, and as he debated what to do for the best he heard a terrific commotion coming from downstairs and went out to the hallway to look over the banister.

Down below he saw the door to Father's office standing open and a group of five men outside it, laughing and shaking hands. Father was at the centre of them and looked very smart in his freshly pressed uniform. His thick dark hair had obviously been recently lacquered and combed, and as Bruno watched from above he felt both scared and in awe of him. He didn't like the look of the other men quite as much. They certainly weren't as handsome as Father. Nor were their uniforms as freshly pressed. Nor were their voices so booming or their boots so polished. They all held their caps under their arms and seemed to be fighting with each other for Father's attention. Bruno could only understand a few of their phrases as they travelled up to him.

'. . . made mistakes from the moment he got here. It got to the point where the Fury had no choice but to . . .' said one.

'. . . discipline!' said another. 'And efficiency. We have lacked efficiency since the start of 'forty-two and without that . . .'

'. . . it's clear, it's clear what the numbers say. It's clear, Commandant . . .' said the third.

'. . . and if we build another,' said the last, 'imagine what we could do then . . . just imagine it . . . !'

Father held a hand in the air, which immediately caused the other men to fall silent. It was as if he was the conductor of a barbershop quartet.

'Gentlemen,' he said, and this time Bruno could make out every word because there had never been a man born who was more capable of being heard from one side of a room to the other than Father. 'Your suggestions and your encouragement are very much appreciated. And the past is the past. Here we have a fresh beginning, but let that beginning start tomorrow. For now, I'd better help my family settle in or there will be as much trouble for me in here as there is for them out there, you understand?'

The men all broke into laughter and shook Father's hand. As they left they stood in a row together like toy soldiers and their arms shot out in the same way that Father had taught Bruno to salute, the palm stretched flat, moving from their chests up into the air in front of them in a sharp motion as they cried out the two words that Bruno had been taught to say whenever anyone said it to him. Then they left and Father returned to his office, which was Out Of Bounds At All Times And No Exceptions.

Bruno walked slowly down the stairs and hesitated for a moment outside the door. He felt sad that Father had not come up to say hello to him in the hour or so that he had been here, but it had been explained to him on many occasions just how busy Father was and that he couldn't be disturbed by silly things like saying hello to him all the time. But the soldiers had left now and he thought it would be all right if he knocked on the door.

Back in Berlin, Bruno had been inside Father's office on only a handful of occasions, and it was usually because he had been naughty and needed to have a serious talking-to. However, the rule that applied to Father's office in Berlin was one of the most important rules that Bruno had ever learned and he was not so silly as to think that it would not apply here at Out-With too. But since they had not seen each other in some days, he thought that no one would mind if he knocked now.

And so he tapped carefully on the door. Twice, and quietly.

Perhaps Father didn't hear, perhaps Bruno didn't knock loudly enough, but no one came to the door, so Bruno knocked again and did it louder this time, and as he did so he heard the booming voice from inside call out, 'Enter!'

Bruno turned the door handle and stepped inside and assumed his customary pose of wide-open eyes, mouth in the shape of an O and arms stretched out by his sides. The rest of the house might have been a little dark and gloomy and hardly full of possibilities for exploration but this room was something else. It had a very high ceiling to begin with, and a carpet underfoot that Bruno thought he might sink into. The walls were hardly visible; instead they were covered with dark mahogany shelves, all lined with books, like the ones in the library at the house in Berlin. There were enormous windows on the wall facing him, which stretched out into the garden beyond, allowing a comfortable seat to be placed in front of them, and in the centre of all this, seated behind a massive oak desk, was Father himself, who looked up from his papers when Bruno entered and broke into a wide smile.

'Bruno,' he said, coming round from behind the desk and shaking the boy's hand solidly, for Father was not usually the type of man to give anyone a hug, unlike Mother and Grandmother, who gave them a little too often for comfort, complementing them with slobbering kisses. 'My boy,' he added after a moment.

'Hello, Father,' said Bruno quietly, a little overawed by the splendour of the room.

'Bruno, I was coming up to see you in a few minutes, I promise I was,' said Father. 'I just had a meeting to finish and a letter to write. You got here safely then?'

'Yes, Father,' said Bruno.

'You were a help to your mother and sister in closing the house?'

'Yes, Father,' said Bruno.

'Then I'm proud of you,' said Father approvingly. 'Sit down, boy.'

He indicated a wide armchair facing his desk and Bruno clambered onto it, his feet not quite touching the floor, while Father returned to his seat behind the desk and stared at him. They didn't say anything to each other for a moment, and then finally Father broke the silence.

'So?' he asked. 'What do you think?'

'What do I think?' asked Bruno. 'What do I think of what?'

'Of your new home. Do you like it?'

'No,' said Bruno quickly, because he always tried to be honest and knew that if he hesitated even for a moment then he wouldn't have the nerve to say what he really thought. 'I think we should go home,' he added bravely.

Father's smile faded only a little and he glanced down at his letter for a moment before looking back up again, as if he wanted to consider his reply

46

carefully. 'Well, we are home, Bruno,' he said finally in a gentle voice. 'Out-With is our new home.'

'But when can we go back to Berlin?' asked Bruno, his heart sinking when Father said that. 'It's so much nicer there.'

'Come, come,' said Father, wanting to have none of that. 'Let's have none of that,' he said. 'A home is not a building or a street or a city or something so artificial as bricks and mortar. A home is where one's family is, isn't that right?'

'Yes, but—'

'And our family is here, Bruno. At Out-With. *Ergo*, this must be our home.'

Bruno didn't understand what *ergo* meant, but he didn't need to because he had a clever answer for Father. 'But Grandfather and Grandmother are in Berlin,' he said. 'And they're our family too. So this can't be our home.'

Father considered this and nodded his head. He waited a long time before replying. 'Yes, Bruno, they are. But you and I and Mother and Gretel are the most important people in our family and this is where we live now. At Out-With. Now, don't look so unhappy about it!' (Because Bruno was looking distinctly unhappy about it.) 'You haven't even given it a chance yet. You might like it here.'

'I don't like it here,' insisted Bruno.

'Bruno . . .' said Father in a tired voice.

'Karl's not here and Daniel's not here and Martin's not here and there are no other houses around us and no fruit and vegetable stalls and no streets and no cafés with tables outside and no one to push you from pillar to post on a Saturday afternoon.'

'Bruno, sometimes there are things we need to do in life that we don't have a choice in,' said Father, and Bruno could tell that he was starting to tire of this conversation. 'And I'm afraid this is one of them. This is my work, important work. Important to our country. Important to the Fury. You'll understand that some day.'

'I want to go home,' said Bruno. He could feel tears welling up behind his eyes and wanted nothing more than for Father to realize just how awful a place Out-With really was and agree that it was time to leave.

'You need to realize that you *are* at home,' he said instead, disappointing Bruno. 'This is it for the fore-seeable future.'

Bruno closed his eyes for a moment. There hadn't been many times in his life when he had been quite so insistent on having his own way and he had certainly never gone to Father with quite so much desire for him to change his mind about something, but the idea of staying here, the idea of having to live in such a horrible place where there was no one at all to play with, was too much to think about. When he opened his eyes again a moment later, Father stepped round from behind his desk and settled himself in an armchair beside him. Bruno watched as he opened a silver case, took out a cigarette and tapped it on the desk before lighting it.

'I remember when I was a child,' said Father, 'there were certain things that I didn't want to do, but when my father said that it would be better for everyone if I did them, I just put my best foot forward and got on with them.'

'What kinds of things?' asked Bruno.

'Oh, I don't know,' said Father, shrugging his shoulders. 'It's neither here nor there anyway. I was just a child and didn't know what was for the best. Sometimes, for example, I didn't want to stay at home and finish my schoolwork; I wanted to be out on the streets, playing with my friends just like you do, and I look back now and see how foolish I was.'

'So you know how I feel,' said Bruno hopefully.

'Yes, but I also knew that my father, your grandfather, knew what was best for me and that I was always happiest when I just accepted that. Do you think that I would have made such a success of my life if I hadn't learned when to argue and when to keep my mouth shut and follow orders? Well, Bruno? Do you?'

Bruno looked around. His gaze landed on the

window in the corner of the room and through it he could see the awful landscape beyond.

'Did you do something wrong?' he asked after a moment. 'Something that made the Fury angry?'

'Me?' said Father, looking at him in surprise. 'What do you mean?'

'Did you do something bad in work? I know that everyone says you're an important man and that the Fury has big things in mind for you, but he'd hardly send you to a place like this if you hadn't done something that he wanted to punish you for.'

Father laughed, which upset Bruno even more; there was nothing that made him more angry than when a grown-up laughed at him for not knowing something, especially when he was trying to find out the answer by asking questions.

'You don't understand the significance of such a position,' Father said.

'Well, I don't think you can have been very good at your job if it means we all have to move away from a very nice home and our friends and come to a horrible place like this. I think you must have done something wrong and you should go and apologize to the Fury and maybe that will be an end to it. Maybe he'll forgive you if you're very sincere about it.'

The words were out before he could really think about whether they were sensible or not; once he heard them floating in the air they didn't seem like entirely the kind of things he should be saying to Father, but there they were, already said, and not a thing he could do to take them back. Bruno swallowed nervously and, after a few moments' silence, glanced back at Father, who was staring at him stony-faced. Bruno licked his lips and looked away. He felt it would be a bad idea to hold Father's eye.

After a few silent and uncomfortable minutes Father stood up slowly from the seat beside him and walked back behind the desk, laying his cigarette on an ashtray.

'I wonder if you are being very brave,' he said quietly after a moment, as if he was debating the matter in his head, 'rather than merely disrespectful. Perhaps that's not such a bad thing.'

'I didn't mean—'

'But you will be quiet now,' said Father, raising his voice and interrupting him because none of the rules of normal family life ever applied to him. 'I have been very considerate of your feelings here, Bruno, because I know that this move is difficult for you. And I have listened to what you have to say, even though your youth and inexperience force you to phrase things in an insolent manner. And you'll notice that I have not reacted to any of this. But the moment has come when you will simply have to accept that—'

'I don't want to accept it!' shouted Bruno, blinking in surprise because he hadn't known he was going to shout out loud. (In fact it came as a complete surprise to him.) He tensed slightly and got ready to make a run for it if necessary. But nothing seemed to be making Father angry today – and if Bruno was honest with himself he would have admitted that Father rarely became angry; he became quiet and distant and always had his way in the end anyway – and rather than shouting at him or chasing him around the house, he simply shook his head and indicated that their debate was at an end.

'Go to your room, Bruno,' he said in such a quiet voice that Bruno knew that he meant business now, so he stood up, tears of frustration forming in his eyes. He walked towards the door, but before opening it he turned round and asked one final question. 'Father?' he began.

'Bruno, I'm not going to—' began Father irritably.

'It's not about that,' said Bruno quickly. 'I just have one other question.'

Father sighed but indicated that he should ask it and then that would be an end to the matter and no arguments.

Bruno thought about his question, wanting to phrase it exactly right this time, just in case it came out as being rude or unco-operative. 'Who are all those people outside?' he said finally.

Father tilted his head to the left, looking a little confused by the question. 'Soldiers, Bruno,' he said. 'And secretaries. Staff workers. You've seen them all before, of course.'

'No, not them,' said Bruno. 'The people I see from my window. In the huts, in the distance. They're all dressed the same.'

'Ah, those people,' said Father, nodding his head and smiling slightly. 'Those people . . . well, they're not people at all, Bruno.'

Bruno frowned. 'They're not?' he asked, unsure what Father meant by that.

'Well, at least not as we understand the term,' Father continued. 'But you shouldn't be worrying about them right now. They're nothing to do with you. You have nothing whatsoever in common with them. Just settle into your new home and be good, that's all I ask. Accept the situation in which you find yourself and everything will be so much easier.'

'Yes, Father,' said Bruno, unsatisfied by the response.

He opened the door and Father called him back for a moment, standing up and raising an eyebrow as if he'd forgotten something. Bruno remembered the moment his father made the signal, and said the phrase and imitated him exactly.

He pushed his two feet together and shot his right arm into the air before clicking his two heels together

and saying in as deep and clear a voice as possible –
as much like Father's as he could manage – the words
he said every time he left a soldier's presence.

'*Heil Hitler*,' he said, which, he presumed, was
another way of saying, 'Well, goodbye for now, have
a pleasant afternoon.'

Chapter Six

The Overpaid Maid

Some days later Bruno was lying on the bed in his room, staring at the ceiling above his head. The white paint was cracked and peeling away from itself in a most unpleasant manner, unlike the paintwork in the house in Berlin, which was never chipped and received an annual top-up every summer when Mother brought the decorators in. On this particular afternoon he lay there and stared at the spidery cracks, narrowing his eyes to consider what might lie behind them. He imagined that there were insects living in the spaces between the paint and the ceiling itself which were pushing it out, cracking it wide, opening it up, trying to create a gap so that they could squeeze through and look for a window where they might make their escape. Nothing, thought Bruno, not even the insects, would ever choose to stay at Out-With.

'Everything here is horrible,' he said out loud, even though there was no one present to hear him, but somehow it made him feel better to hear the words stated anyway. 'I hate this house, I hate my room and I even hate the paintwork. I hate it all. Absolutely everything.'

Just as he finished speaking Maria came through the door carrying an armful of his washed, dried and ironed clothes. She hesitated for a moment when she saw him lying there but then bowed her head a little and walked silently over towards the wardrobe.

'Hello,' said Bruno, for although talking to a maid wasn't quite the same thing as having some friends to talk to, there was no one else around to have a conversation with and it made much more sense than talking to himself. Gretel was nowhere to be found and he had begun to worry that he would go mad with boredom.

'Master Bruno,' said Maria quietly, separating his vests from his trousers and his underwear and putting them in different drawers and on different shelves.

'I expect you're as unhappy about this new arrangement as I am,' said Bruno, and she turned to look at him with an expression that suggested she didn't understand what he meant. 'This,' he explained, sitting up and looking around. 'Everything here. It's awful, isn't it? Don't you hate it too?'

Maria opened her mouth to say something and

then closed it again just as quickly. She seemed to be considering her response carefully, selecting the right words, preparing to say them, and then thinking better of it and discarding them altogether. Bruno had known her for almost all his life – she had come to work for them when he was only three years old – and they had always got along quite well for the most part, but she had never showed any particular signs of life before. She just got on with her job, polishing the furniture, washing the clothes, helping with the shopping and the cooking, sometimes taking him to school and collecting him again, although that had been more common when Bruno was eight; when he turned nine he decided he was old enough to make his way there and home alone.

'Don't you like it here then?' she said finally.

'Like it?' replied Bruno with a slight laugh. 'Like it?' he repeated, but louder this time. 'Of course I don't like it! It's awful. There's nothing to do, there's no one to talk to, nobody to play with. You can't tell me that you're happy we've moved here, surely?'

'I always enjoyed the garden at the house in Berlin,' said Maria, answering an entirely different question. 'Sometimes, when it was a warm afternoon, I liked to sit out there in the sunshine and eat my lunch underneath the ivy tree by the pond. The flowers were very beautiful there. The scents.

The way the bees hovered around them and never bothered you if you just left them alone.'

'So you don't like it here then?' asked Bruno. 'You think it's as bad as I do?'

Maria frowned. 'It's not important,' she said.

'What isn't?'

'What I think.'

'Well, of course it's important,' said Bruno irritably, as if she was just being deliberately difficult. 'You're part of the family, aren't you?'

'I'm not sure whether your father would agree with that,' said Maria, allowing herself a smile because she was touched by what he had just said.

'Well, you've been brought here against your will, just like I have. If you ask me, we're all in the same boat. And it's leaking.'

For a moment it seemed to Bruno as if Maria really was going to tell him what she was thinking. She laid the rest of his clothes down on the bed and her hands clenched into fists, as if she was terribly angry about something. Her mouth opened but froze there for a moment, as if she was scared of all the things she might say if she allowed herself to begin.

'Please tell me, Maria,' said Bruno. 'Because maybe if we all feel the same way we can persuade Father to take us home again.'

She looked away from him for a few silent moments and shook her head sadly before turning back to face him. 'Your father knows what is for the best,' she said. 'You must trust in that.'

'But I'm not sure I do,' said Bruno. 'I think he's made a terrible mistake.'

'Then it's a mistake we all have to live with.'

'When I make mistakes I get punished,' insisted Bruno, irritated by the fact that the rules that always applied to children never seemed to apply to grown-ups at all (despite the fact that they were the ones who enforced them). 'Stupid Father,' he added under his breath.

Maria's eyes opened wide and she took a step towards him, her hands covering her mouth for a moment in horror. She looked round to make sure that no one was listening to them and had heard what Bruno had just said. 'You mustn't say that,' she said. 'You must never say something like that about your father.'

'I don't see why not,' said Bruno; he was a little ashamed of himself for having said it, but the last thing he was going to do was sit back and receive a telling-off when no one seemed to care about his opinions anyway.

'Because your father is a good man,' said Maria. 'A very good man. He takes care of all of us.'

'Bringing us all the way out here, to the middle of nowhere, you mean? Is that taking care of us?'

'There are many things your father has done,' she

said. 'Many things of which you should be proud. If it wasn't for your father, where would I be now after all?'

'Back in Berlin, I expect,' said Bruno. 'Working in a nice house. Eating your lunch underneath the ivy and leaving the bees alone.'

'You don't remember when I came to work for you, do you?' she asked quietly, sitting down for a moment on the side of his bed, something she had never done before. 'How could you? You were only three. Your father took me in and helped me when I needed him. He gave me a job, a home. Food. You can't imagine what it's like to need food. You've never been hungry, have you?'

Bruno frowned. He wanted to mention that he was feeling a bit peckish right now, but instead he looked across at Maria and realized for the first time that he had never fully considered her to be a person with a life and a history all of her own. After all, she had never done anything (as far as he knew) other than be his family's maid. He wasn't even sure that he had ever seen her dressed in anything other than her maid's uniform. But when he came to think of it, as he did now, he had to admit that there must be more to her life than just waiting on him and his family. She must have thoughts in her head, just like him. She must have things that she missed, friends whom she wanted to see again, just like him. And she must have cried herself to sleep every night since she got here, just like boys far less grown up and brave than him. She was rather pretty too, he noticed, feeling a little funny inside as he did so.

'My mother knew your father when he was just a boy of your age,' said Maria after a few moments. 'She worked for your grandmother. She was a dresser for her when she toured Germany as a younger woman. She arranged all the clothes for her concerts – washed them, ironed them, repaired them. Magnificent gowns, all of them. And the stitching, Bruno! Like art work, every design. You don't find dressmakers like that these days.' She shook her head and smiled at the memory as Bruno listened patiently. 'She made sure that they were all laid out and ready whenever your grandmother arrived in her dressing room before a show. And after your grandmother retired, of course my mother stayed friendly with her and received a small pension, but times were hard then and your father offered me a job, the first I had ever had. A few months later my mother became very sick and she needed a lot of hospital care and your father arranged it all, even though he was not obliged to. He paid for it out of his own pocket because she had been a friend to his mother. And he took me into his household for the same reason. And when she died he paid all the expenses for her funeral too. So don't you ever call your father stupid, Bruno. Not around me. I won't allow it.'

Bruno bit his lip. He had hoped that Maria would take his side in the campaign to get away from Out-With but he could see where her loyalties really lay. And he had to admit that he was rather proud of his father when he heard that story.

'Well,' he said, unable to think of something clever to say now, 'I suppose that was nice of him.'

'Yes,' said Maria, standing up and walking over towards the window, the one through which Bruno could see all the way to the huts and the people in the distance. 'He was very kind to me then,' she continued quietly, looking through it herself now and watching the people and the soldiers go about their business far away. 'He has a lot of kindness in his soul, truly he does, which makes me wonder . . .' She drifted off as she watched them and her voice cracked suddenly and she sounded as if she might cry.

'Wonder what?' asked Bruno.

'Wonder what he . . . how he can . . .'

'How he can *what*?' insisted Bruno.

The noise of a door slamming came from downstairs and reverberated through the house so loudly – like a gunshot – that Bruno jumped and Maria let out a small scream. Bruno recognized footsteps pounding up the stairs towards them, quicker and quicker, and he crawled back on the bed, pressing himself against the wall, suddenly afraid of what was going to happen next. He held his breath, expecting trouble, but it was only Gretel, the Hopeless Case. She poked her head through the doorway and seemed surprised to find her brother and the family maid engaged in conversation.

'What's going on?' asked Gretel.

'Nothing,' said Bruno defensively. 'What do you want? Get out.'

'Get out yourself,' she replied even though it was his room, and then turned to look at Maria, narrowing her eyes suspiciously as she did so. 'Run me a bath, Maria, will you?' she asked.

'Why can't you run your own bath?' snapped Bruno.

'Because she's the maid,' said Gretel, staring at him. 'That's what she's here for.'

'That's *not* what she's here for,' shouted Bruno, standing up and marching over to her. 'She's not just here to do things for us all the time, you know. Especially things that we can do ourselves.'

Gretel stared at him as if he had gone mad and then looked at Maria, who shook her head quickly.

'Of course, Miss Gretel,' said Maria. 'I'll just finish tidying your brother's clothes away and I'll be right with you.'

'Well, don't be long,' said Gretel rudely – because unlike Bruno she never stopped to think about the fact that Maria was a person with feelings just like hers – before marching off back to her room and closing the door behind her. Maria's eyes didn't follow her but her cheeks had taken on a pink glow.

'I still think he's made a terrible mistake,' said Bruno quietly after a few minutes when he felt as if he wanted to apologize for his sister's behaviour but didn't know whether that was the right thing to do or not. Situations like that always made Bruno feel very uncomfortable because, in his heart, he knew that there was no reason to be impolite to someone, even if they did work for you. There was such a thing as manners after all.

'Even if you do, you mustn't say it out loud,' said Maria quickly, coming towards him and looking as if she wanted to shake some sense into him. 'Promise me you won't.'

'But why?' he asked, frowning. 'I'm only saying what I feel. I'm allowed to do that, aren't I?'

'No,' she said. 'No, you're not.'

'I'm not allowed to say what I feel?' he repeated, incredulous.

'No,' she insisted, her voice becoming grating now as she appealed to him. 'Just keep quiet about it, Bruno. Don't you know how much trouble you could cause? For all of us?'

Bruno stared at her. There was something in her eyes, a sort of frenzied worry, that he had never seen there before and that unsettled him. 'Well,' he muttered, standing up now and heading over towards the door, suddenly anxious to be away from her, 'I was only saying I didn't like it here, that's all. I was just making conversation while you put the clothes away. It's not like I'm planning on running away or anything. Although if I did I don't think anyone could criticize me for it.'

'And worry your mother and father half to death?' asked Maria. 'Bruno, if you have any sense at all, you will stay quiet and concentrate on your school work and do whatever your father tells you. We must all just keep ourselves safe until this is all over. That's what I intend to do anyway. What more can we do than that after all? It's not up to us to change things.'

Suddenly, and for no reason that he could think of, Bruno felt an overwhelming urge to cry. It surprised even him and he blinked a few times very quickly so that Maria wouldn't see how he felt. Although when he caught her eye again he thought that perhaps there must be something strange in the air that day because her eyes looked as if they were filling with tears too. All in all, he began to feel very awkward, so he turned his back on her and made his way to the door.

'Where are you going?' asked Maria.

'Outside,' said Bruno angrily. 'If it's any of your business.'

He had walked slowly but once he left the room he went more quickly towards the stairs and then ran down them at a great pace, suddenly feeling that if he didn't get out of the house soon he was going to faint away. And within a few seconds he was outside and he started to run up and down the driveway, eager to do something active, anything that would tire him out. In the distance he could see the gate that led to the road that led to the train station that led home, but the idea of going there, the idea of running away and being left on his own without anyone at all, was even more unpleasant to him than the idea of staying.

Chapter Seven

How Mother Took Credit for Something That
She Hadn't Done

Several weeks after Bruno arrived at Out-With with his family and with no prospect of a visit on the horizon from either Karl or Daniel or Martin, he decided that he'd better start to find some way to entertain himself or he would slowly go mad.

Bruno had only known one person whom he considered to be mad and that was Herr Roller, a man of about the same age as Father, who lived round the corner from him back at the old house in Berlin. He was often seen walking up and down the street at all hours of the day or night, having terrible arguments with himself. Sometimes, in the middle of these arguments, the dispute would get out of hand and he would try to punch the shadow he was throwing up against the wall. From time to time he fought so hard that he banged his fists against the brickwork and they bled and then he would fall onto his knees and start crying loudly and slapping his hands against his head. On a few occasions Bruno had heard him using those words that he wasn't allowed to use, and when he did this Bruno had to stop himself from giggling.

'You shouldn't laugh at poor Herr Roller,' Mother had told him one afternoon when he had related the story of his latest escapade. 'You have no idea what he's been through in his life.'

'He's crazy,' Bruno said, twirling a finger in circles around the side of his head and whistling to indicate just how crazy he thought he was. 'He went up to a cat on the street the other day and invited her over for afternoon tea.'

'What did the cat say?' asked Gretel, who was making a sandwich in the corner of the kitchen.

'Nothing,' explained Bruno. 'It was a cat.'

'I mean it,' Mother insisted. 'Franz was a very lovely young man – I knew him when I was a little girl. He was kind and thoughtful and could make his way around a dance floor like Fred Astaire. But he suffered a terrible injury during the Great War, an injury to his head, and that's why he behaves as he does now. It's nothing to laugh at. You have no idea of what the young men went through back then. Their suffering.'

Bruno had only been six years old at the time and wasn't quite sure what Mother was referring to. 'It was many years ago,' she explained when he asked her about it. 'Before you were born. Franz was one of the young men who fought for us in the trenches. Your father knew him very well back then; I believe they served together.'

'And what happened to him?' asked Bruno.

'It doesn't matter,' said Mother. 'War is not a fit subject for conversation. I'm afraid we'll be spending too much time talking about it soon.'

That had been just over three years before they all arrived at Out-With and Bruno hadn't spent much time thinking about Herr Roller in the meantime, but he suddenly became convinced that if he didn't do something sensible, something to put his mind to some use, then before he knew it he would be wandering around the streets having fights with himself and inviting domestic animals to social occasions too.

To keep himself entertained Bruno spent a long Saturday morning and afternoon creating a new diversion for himself. At some distance from the house – on Gretel's side and impossible to see from his own bedroom window – there was a large oak tree, one with a very wide trunk. A tall tree with hefty branches, strong enough to support a small boy. It looked so old that Bruno decided it must have been planted at some point in the late Middle Ages, a period he had recently been studying and was finding very interesting – particularly those parts about knights who went off on adventures to foreign lands and discovered something interesting while they were there.

There were only two things that Bruno needed to create his new entertainment: some rope and a tyre. The rope was easy enough to find as there were bales of it in the basement of the house and it didn't take long to do something extremely dangerous and find a sharp knife and cut as many lengths of it as he thought he might need. He took these to the oak tree and left them on the ground for future use. The tyre was another matter.

On this particular morning neither Mother nor Father was at home. Mother had rushed out of the house early and taken a train to a nearby city for the day for a change of air, while Father had last been seen heading in the direction of the huts and the people in the distance outside Bruno's window. But as usual there were many soldiers' trucks and jeeps parked near the house, and while he knew it would be impossible to steal a tyre off any of them, there was always the possibility that he could find a spare one somewhere.

As he stepped outside he saw Gretel speaking with Lieutenant Kotler and, without much enthusiasm, decided that he would be the sensible person to ask. Lieutenant Kotler was the young officer whom Bruno had seen on his very first day at Out-With, the soldier who had appeared upstairs in their house and looked at him for a moment before nodding his head and continuing on his way. Bruno had seen him on many occasions since – he came in and out of the house as if he owned the place and Father's office was clearly not out of bounds to him at all – but they hadn't spoken very often. Bruno wasn't entirely sure why, but he knew that he didn't like Lieutenant Kotler. There was an atmosphere around him that made Bruno feel very cold and want to put a jumper on. Still, there was no one else to ask so he marched over with as much confidence as he could muster to say hello.

On most days the young lieutenant looked very smart, striding around in a uniform that appeared to have been ironed while he was wearing it. His black boots always sparkled with polish and his yellow-blond hair was parted at the side and held perfectly in place with something that made all the comb marks stand out in it, like a field that had just been tilled. Also he wore so much cologne that you could smell him coming from quite a distance. Bruno had learned not to stand downwind of him or he would risk fainting away.

On this particular day, however, since it was a Saturday morning and was so sunny, he was not so perfectly groomed. Instead he was wearing a white vest over his trousers and his hair flopped down over his forehead in exhaustion. His arms were surprisingly tanned and he had the kind of muscles that Bruno wished he had himself. He looked so much younger today that Bruno was surprised; in fact he reminded him of the big boys at school, the ones he always steered clear of. Lieutenant Kotler was deep in conversation with Gretel and whatever he was saying must have been terribly funny because she was laughing loudly and twirling her hair around her fingers into ringlets.

'Hello,' said Bruno as he approached them, and Gretel looked at him irritably.

'What do *you* want?' she asked.

'I don't *want* anything,' snapped Bruno, glaring at her. 'I just came over to say hello.'

'You'll have to forgive my younger brother, Kurt,' said Gretel to Lieutenant Kotler. 'He's only nine, you know.'

'Good morning, little man,' said Kotler, reaching out and – quite appallingly – ruffling his hand through Bruno's hair, a gesture that made Bruno want to push him to the ground and jump up and down on his head. 'And what has you up and about so early on a Saturday morning?'

'It's hardly early,' said Bruno. 'It's almost ten o'clock.'

Lieutenant Kotler shrugged his shoulders. 'When I was your age my mother couldn't get me out of bed until lunch time. She said I would never grow up to be big and strong if I slept my life away.'

'Well, she was quite wrong there, wasn't she?' simpered Gretel. Bruno stared at her with distaste. She was putting on a silly voice that made her sound as if she hadn't a thought in her head. There was nothing Bruno wanted to do more than walk away from the two of them and have nothing to do with whatever they were discussing, but he had no choice but to put his best interests first and ask Lieutenant Kotler for the unthinkable. A favour.

'I wondered if I could ask you a favour,' said Bruno.

'You can ask,' said Lieutenant Kotler, which made Gretel laugh again even though it was not particularly funny.

'I wondered whether there were any spare tyres around,' Bruno continued. 'From one of the jeeps perhaps. Or a truck. One that you're not using.'

'The only spare tyre I have seen around here recently belongs to Sergeant Hoffschneider, and he carries it around his waist,' said Lieutenant Kotler, his lips forming into something that resembled a smile. This didn't make any sense at all to Bruno, but it entertained Gretel so much that she appeared to start dancing on the spot.

'Well, is he using it?' asked Bruno.

'Sergeant Hoffschneider?' asked Lieutenant Kotler. 'Yes, I'm afraid so. He's very attached to his spare tyre.'

'Stop it, Kurt,' said Gretel, drying her eyes. 'He doesn't understand you. He's only nine.'

'Oh, will you be quiet please,' shouted Bruno, staring at his sister in irritation. It was bad enough having to come out here and ask for a favour from Lieutenant Kotler, but it only made things worse when his own sister teased him all the way through it. 'You're only twelve anyway,' he added. 'So stop pretending to be older than you are.'

'I'm nearly thirteen, Kurt,' she snapped, her laughter stopped now, her face frozen in horror. 'I'll be thirteen in a couple of weeks' time. A teenager. Just like you.'

Lieutenant Kotler smiled and nodded his head but said nothing. Bruno stared at him. If it had been any other adult standing in front of him he would have rolled his eyes to suggest that they both knew that girls were silly, and sisters utterly ridiculous. But this wasn't any other adult. This was Lieutenant Kotler.

'Anyway,' said Bruno, ignoring the look of anger that Gretel was directing towards him, 'other than that one, is there anywhere else that I could find a spare tyre?'

'Of course,' said Lieutenant Kotler, who had stopped smiling now and seemed suddenly bored with the entire thing. 'But what do you want it for anyway?'

'I thought I'd make a swing,' said Bruno. 'You

know, with a tyre and some rope on the branches of a tree.'

'Indeed,' said Lieutenant Kotler, nodding his head wisely as if such things were only distant memories to him now, despite the fact that he was, as Gretel had pointed out, no more than a teenager himself. 'Yes, I made many swings myself when I was a child. My friends and I had many happy afternoons together playing on them.'

Bruno felt astonished that he could have anything in common with him (and even more surprised to learn that Lieutenant Kotler had ever had friends). 'So what do you think?' he asked. 'Are there any around?'

Lieutenant Kotler stared at him and seemed to be considering it, as if he wasn't sure whether he was going to give him a straight answer or try to irritate him as he usually did. Then he caught sight of Pavel – the old man who came every afternoon to help peel the vegetables in the kitchen for dinner before putting his white jacket on and serving at the table – heading towards the house, and this seemed to make his mind up.

'Hey, you!' he shouted, then adding a word that Bruno did not understand. 'Come over here, you—' He said the word again, and something about the harsh sound of it made Bruno look away and feel ashamed to be part of this at all.

Pavel came towards them and Kotler spoke to him insolently, despite the fact that he was young enough to be his grandson. 'Take this little man to the storage shed at the back of the main house. Lined up along a side wall are some old tyres. He will select one and you are to carry it wherever he asks you to, is that understood?'

Pavel held his cap before him in his hands and nodded, which made his head bow even lower than it already was. 'Yes, sir,' he said in a quiet voice, so quiet that he may not even have said it at all.

'And afterwards, when you return to the kitchen, make sure you wash your hands before touching any of the food, you filthy—' Lieutenant Kotler repeated the word he had used twice already and he spat a little as he spoke. Bruno glanced across at Gretel, who had been staring adoringly at the sunlight bouncing off Lieutenant Kotler's hair but now, like her brother, looked a little uncomfortable. Neither of them had ever really spoken to Pavel before but he was a very good waiter and they, according to Father, did not grow on trees.

'Off you go then,' said Lieutenant Kotler, and Pavel turned and led the way towards the storage shed, followed by Bruno, who from time to time glanced back in the direction of his sister and the young soldier and felt a great urge to go back there and pull Gretel away, despite the fact that she was

annoying and self-centred and mean to him most of
the time. That, after all, was her job. She was his
sister. But he hated the idea of leaving her alone with
a man like Lieutenant Kotler. There really was no
other way to dress it up: he was just plain nasty.

The accident took place a couple of hours later after
Bruno had located a suitable tyre and Pavel had
dragged it to the large oak tree on Gretel's side of the
house, and after Bruno had climbed up and down
and up and down and up and down the trunk to tie
the ropes securely around the branches and the tyre
itself. Until then the whole operation had been a
tremendous success. He had built one of these once
before, but back then he had had Karl and Daniel
and Martin to help him with it. On this occasion he
was doing it by himself and that made things
decidedly trickier. And yet somehow he managed it,
and within a few hours he was happily installed
inside the centre of the tyre and swinging back and
forth as if he did not have a care in the world,
although he was ignoring the fact that it was one of
the most uncomfortable swings he had ever been on
in his life.

He lay flat out across the centre of the tyre and
used his feet to give himself a good push off the
ground. Every time the tyre swung backwards it rose
in the air and narrowly avoided hitting the trunk of

the tree itself, but it still came close enough for Bruno to use his feet to kick himself even faster and higher on the next swing. This worked very well until his grip on the tyre slipped a little just as he kicked the tree, and before he knew it his body was turning inside and he fell downwards, one foot still inside the rim while he landed face down on the ground beneath him with a thud.

Everything went black for a moment and then came back into focus. He sat up on the ground just as the tyre swung back and hit him on the head and he let out a yelp and moved out of its way. When he stood up he could feel that his arm and leg were both very sore as he had fallen heavily on them, but they weren't so sore that they might be broken. He inspected his hand and it was covered in scratches and when he looked at his elbow he could see a nasty cut. His leg felt worse though, and when he looked down at his knee, just below where his shorts ended, there was a wide gash which seemed to have been waiting for him to look at it because once all the attention was focused on it, it started to bleed rather badly.

'Oh dear,' said Bruno out loud, staring at it and wondering what he should do next. He didn't have to wonder for long though, because the swing that he had built was on the same side of the house as the kitchen, and Pavel, the waiter who had helped him find the tyre, had been peeling potatoes while standing at the window and had seen the accident take place. When Bruno looked up again he saw Pavel coming quickly towards him, and only when he arrived did he feel confident enough to let the woozy feeling that was surrounding him take him over completely. He fell a little but didn't land on the ground this time, as Pavel scooped him up.

'I don't know what happened,' he said. 'It didn't seem dangerous at all.'

'You were going too high,' said Pavel in a quiet voice that immediately made Bruno feel safe. 'I could see it. I thought that at any moment you were going to suffer a mischief.'

'And I did,' said Bruno.

'You certainly did.'

Pavel carried him across the lawn and back towards the house, taking him into the kitchen and settling him on one of the wooden chairs.

'Where's Mother?' asked Bruno, looking around for the first person he usually searched for when he'd had an accident.

'Your mother hasn't returned yet, I'm afraid,' said Pavel, who was kneeling on the floor in front of him and examining the knee. 'I'm the only one here.'

'What's going to happen then?' asked Bruno, beginning to panic slightly, an emotion that might encourage tears. 'I might bleed to death.'

Pavel gave a gentle laugh and shook his head. 'You're not going to bleed to death,' he said, pulling a stool across and settling Bruno's leg on it. 'Don't move for a moment. There's a first-aid box over here.'

Bruno watched as he moved around the kitchen, pulling the green first-aid box from a cupboard and filling a small bowl with water, testing it first with his finger to make sure that it wasn't too cold.

'Will I need to go to hospital?' asked Bruno.

'No, no,' said Pavel when he returned to his kneeling position, dipping a dry cloth into the bowl and touching it gently to Bruno's knee, which made him wince in pain, despite the fact that it wasn't really all that painful. 'It's only a small cut. It won't even need stitches.'

Bruno frowned and bit his lip nervously as Pavel cleaned the wound of blood and then held another cloth to it quite tightly for a few minutes. When he pulled it away again, gently, the bleeding had stopped, and he took a small bottle of green liquid from the first-aid box and dabbed it over the wound, which stung quite sharply and made Bruno say 'Ow' a few times in rapid succession.

'It's not that bad,' said Pavel, but in a gentle and kindly voice. 'Don't make it worse by thinking it's more painful than it actually is.'

Somehow this made sense to Bruno and he resisted

the urge to say 'Ow' any more, and when Pavel had finished applying the green liquid he took a bandage from the first-aid box and taped it to the cut.

'There,' he said. 'All better, eh?'

Bruno nodded and felt a little ashamed of himself for not behaving as bravely as he would have liked. 'Thank you,' he said.

'You're welcome,' said Pavel. 'Now you need to stay sitting there for a few minutes before you walk around on it again, all right? Let the wound relax. And don't go near that swing again today.'

Bruno nodded and kept his leg stretched out on the stool while Pavel went over to the sink and washed his hands carefully, even scrubbing under his nails with a wire brush, before drying them off and returning to the potatoes.

'Will you tell Mother what happened?' asked Bruno, who had spent the last few minutes wondering whether he would be viewed as a hero for suffering an accident or a villain for building a death-trap.

'I think she'll see for herself,' said Pavel, who took the carrots over to the table now and sat down opposite Bruno as he began to peel them onto an old newspaper.

'Yes, I suppose so,' said Bruno. 'Perhaps she'll want to take me to a doctor.'

'I don't think so,' said Pavel quietly.

'You never know,' said Bruno, who didn't want his accident to be dismissed quite so easily. (It was, after all, quite the most exciting thing that had happened to him since arriving here.) 'It could be worse than it seems.'

'It's not,' said Pavel, who barely seemed to be listening to what Bruno was saying, the carrots were taking up so much of his attention.

'Well, how do you know?' asked Bruno quickly, growing irritable now despite the fact that this was the same man who had come out to pick him up off the ground and brought him in and taken care of him. 'You're not a doctor.'

Pavel stopped peeling the carrots for a moment and looked across the table at Bruno, his head held low, his eyes looking up, as if he were wondering what to say to such a thing. He sighed and seemed to consider it for quite a long time before saying, 'Yes I am.'

Bruno stared at him in surprise. This didn't make any sense to him. 'But you're a waiter,' he said slowly. 'And you peel the vegetables for dinner. How can you be a doctor too?'

'Young man,' said Pavel (and Bruno appreciated the fact that he had the courtesy to call him 'young man' instead of 'little man' as Lieutenant Kotler had), 'I certainly am a doctor. Just because a man glances up at the sky at night does not make him an astronomer, you know.'

Bruno had no idea what Pavel meant but something about what he had said made him look at him closely for the first time. He was quite a small man, and very skinny too, with long fingers and angular features. He was older than Father but younger than Grandfather, which still meant he was quite old, and although Bruno had never laid eyes on him before coming to Out-With, something about his face made him believe that he had worn a beard in the past.

But not any more.

'But I don't understand,' said Bruno, wanting to get to the bottom of this. 'If you're a doctor, then why are you waiting on tables? Why aren't you working at a hospital somewhere?'

Pavel hesitated for a long time before answering, and while he did so Bruno said nothing. He wasn't sure why but he felt that the polite thing to do was to wait until Pavel was ready to speak.

'Before I came here, I practised as a doctor,' he said finally.

'Practised?' asked Bruno, who was unfamiliar with the word. 'Weren't you any good then?'

Pavel smiled. 'I was very good,' he said. 'I always wanted to be a doctor, you see. From the time I was a small boy. From the time I was your age.'

'I want to be an explorer,' said Bruno quickly.

'I wish you luck,' said Pavel.

'Thank you.'

'Have you discovered anything yet?'

'Back in our house in Berlin there was a lot of exploring to be done,' recalled Bruno. 'But then, it was a very big house, bigger than you could possibly imagine, so there were a lot of places to explore. It's not the same here.'

'Nothing is the same here,' agreed Pavel.

'When did you arrive at Out-With?' asked Bruno.

Pavel put the carrot and the peeler down for a few moments and thought about it. 'I think I've always been here,' he said finally in a quiet voice.

'You grew up here?'

'No,' said Pavel, shaking his head. 'No, I didn't.'

'But you just said—'

Before he could go on, Mother's voice could be heard outside. As soon as he heard her, Pavel jumped up quickly from his seat and returned to the sink with the carrots and the peeler and the newspaper full of peelings, and turned his back on Bruno, hanging his head low and not speaking again.

'What on earth happened to you?' asked Mother when she appeared in the kitchen, leaning down to examine the plaster which covered Bruno's cut.

'I made a swing and then I fell off it,' explained Bruno. 'And then the swing hit me on the head and I nearly fainted, but Pavel came out and brought me in and cleaned it all up and put a bandage on me and it stung very badly but I didn't cry. I didn't cry once, did I, Pavel?'

Pavel turned his body slightly in their direction but didn't lift his head. 'The wound has been cleaned,' he said quietly, not answering Bruno's question. 'There's nothing to worry about.'

'Go to your room, Bruno,' said Mother, who looked distinctly uncomfortable now.

'But I—'

'Don't argue with me – go to your room!' she insisted, and Bruno stepped off the chair, putting his weight on what he had decided to call his bad leg, and it hurt a little. He turned and left the room but was still able to hear Mother saying thank you to Pavel as he walked towards the stairs, and this made Bruno happy because surely it was obvious to everyone that if it hadn't been for him, he would have bled to death.

He heard one last thing before going upstairs and that was Mother's last line to the waiter who claimed to be a doctor.

'If the Commandant asks, we'll say that I cleaned Bruno up.'

Which seemed terribly selfish to Bruno and a way for Mother to take credit for something that she hadn't done.

Chapter Eight

Why Grandmother Stormed Out

The two people Bruno missed most of all from home were Grandfather and Grandmother. They lived together in a small flat near the fruit and vegetable stalls, and around the time that Bruno moved to Out-With, Grandfather was almost seventy-three years old which, as far as Bruno was concerned, made him just about the oldest man in the world. One afternoon Bruno had calculated that if he lived his entire life over and over again eight times, he would still be a year younger than Grandfather.

Grandfather had spent his entire life running a restaurant in the centre of town, and one of his employees was the father of Bruno's friend Martin who worked there as a chef. Although Grandfather no longer cooked or waited on tables in the restaurant himself, he spent most of his days there, sitting at the bar in the afternoon talking to the customers, eating his meals there in the evening and staying until closing time, laughing with his friends.

Grandmother never seemed old in comparison to the other boys' grandmothers. In fact when Bruno learned just how old she was – sixty-two – he was amazed. She had met Grandfather as a young woman after one of her concerts and somehow he had persuaded her to marry him, despite all his flaws. She had long red hair, surprisingly similar to her daughter-in-law's, and green eyes, and she claimed that was because somewhere in her family there was Irish blood. Bruno always knew when a family party was getting into full swing because Grandmother would hover by the piano until someone sat down at it and asked her to sing.

'What's that?' she always cried, holding a hand to her chest as if the very idea took her breath away. 'Is it a song you're wanting? Why, I couldn't possibly. I'm afraid, young man, my singing days are far behind me.'

'Sing! Sing!' everyone at the party would cry, and after a suitable pause – sometimes as long as ten or twelve seconds – she would finally give in and turn to the young man at the piano and say in a quick and humorous voice:

'*La Vie en Rose*, E-flat minor. And try to keep up with the changes.'

Parties at Bruno's house were always dominated by Grandmother's singing, which for some reason always seemed to coincide with the moment when

Mother moved from the main party area to the kitchen, followed by some of her own friends. Father always stayed to listen and Bruno did too because there was nothing he liked more than hearing Grandmother break into her full voice and soak up the applause of the guests at the end. Plus, *La Vie en Rose* gave him chills and made the tiny hairs on the back of his neck stand on end.

Grandmother liked to think that Bruno or Gretel would follow her onto the stage, and every Christmas and at every birthday party she would devise a small play for the three of them to perform for Mother, Father and Grandfather. She wrote the plays herself and, to Bruno's way of thinking, always gave herself the best lines, though he didn't mind that too much. There was usually a song in there somewhere too – *Is it a song you're wanting?* she'd ask first – and an opportunity for Bruno to do a magic trick and for Gretel to dance. The play always ended with Bruno reciting a long poem by one of the Great Poets, words which he found very hard to understand but which somehow started to sound more and more beautiful the more he read them.

But that wasn't the best part of these little productions. The best part was the fact that Grandmother made costumes for Bruno and Gretel. No matter what the role, no matter how few lines he might have in comparison to his sister or grandmother, Bruno always got to dress up as a prince, or an Arab sheik, or even on one occasion a Roman gladiator. There were crowns, and when there weren't crowns there were spears. And when there weren't spears there were whips or turbans. No one ever knew what Grandmother would come up with next, but a week before Christmas Bruno and Gretel would be summoned to her home on a daily basis for rehearsals.

Of course the last play they performed had ended in disaster and Bruno still remembered it with sadness, although he wasn't quite sure what had happened to cause the argument.

A week or so before, there had been great excitement in the house and it had something to do with the fact that Father was now to be addressed as 'Commandant' by Maria, Cook and Lars the butler, as well as by all the soldiers who came in and out of there and used the place – as far as Bruno could see – as if it were their own and not his. There had been nothing but excitement for weeks. First the Fury and the beautiful blonde woman had come to dinner, which had brought the whole house to a standstill, and then it was this new business of calling Father 'Commandant'. Mother had told Bruno to congratulate Father and he had done so, although if he was honest with himself (which he always tried to be) he wasn't entirely sure what he was congratulating him for.

On Christmas Day Father wore his brand-new uniform, the starched and pressed one that he wore every day now, and the whole family applauded when he first appeared in it. It really was something special. Compared to the other soldiers who came in and out of the house, he stood out, and they seemed to respect him all the more now that he had it. Mother went up to him and kissed him on the cheek and ran a hand across the front of it, commenting on how fine she thought the fabric was. Bruno was particularly impressed by all the decorations on the uniform and he had been allowed to wear the cap for a short period, provided his hands were clean when he put it on.

Grandfather was very proud of his son when he saw him in his new uniform but Grandmother was the only one who seemed unimpressed. After dinner had been served, and after she and Gretel and Bruno had performed their latest production, she sat down sadly in one of the armchairs and looked at Father, shaking her head as if he were a huge disappointment to her.

'I wonder – is this where I went wrong with you, Ralf?' she said. 'I wonder if all the performances I made you give as a boy led you to this. Dressing up like a puppet on a string.'

'Now, Mother,' said Father in a tolerant voice. 'You know this isn't the time.'

'Standing there in your uniform,' she continued, 'as if it makes you something special. Not even caring what it means really. What it stands for.'

'Nathalie, we discussed this in advance,' said Grandfather, although everyone knew that when Grandmother had something to say she always found a way to say it, no matter how unpopular it might prove to be.

'*You* discussed it, Matthias,' said Grandmother. 'I was merely the blank wall to whom you addressed your words. As usual.'

'This is a party, Mother,' said Father with a sigh. 'And it's Christmas. Let's not spoil things.'

'I remember when the Great War began,' said Grandfather proudly, staring into the fire and shaking his head. 'I remember you coming home to tell us how you had joined up and I was sure that you would come to harm.'

'He did come to harm, Matthias,' insisted Grandmother. 'Take a look at him for your evidence.'

'And now look at you,' continued Grandfather, ignoring her. 'It makes me so proud to see you elevated to such a responsible position. Helping your country reclaim her pride after all the great wrongs that were done to her. The punishments above and beyond—'

'Oh, will you listen to yourself!' cried

Grandmother. 'Which one of you is the most foolish, I wonder?'

'But, Nathalie,' said Mother, trying to calm the situation down a little, 'don't you think Ralf looks very handsome in his new uniform?'

'Handsome?' asked Grandmother, leaning forward and staring at her daughter-in-law as if she had lost her reason. 'Handsome, did you say? You foolish girl! Is that what you consider to be of importance in the world? Looking handsome?'

'Do I look handsome in my ringmaster's costume?' asked Bruno, for that was what he had been wearing for the party that night – the red and black outfit of a circus ringmaster – and he had been very proud of himself in it. The moment he spoke he regretted it, however, for all the adults looked in his and Gretel's direction, as if they had forgotten that they were there at all.

'Children, upstairs,' said Mother quickly. 'Go to your rooms.'

'But we don't want to,' protested Gretel. 'Can't we play down here?'

'No, children,' she insisted. 'Go upstairs and close the door behind you.'

'That's all you soldiers are interested in anyway,' Grandmother said, ignoring the children altogether. 'Looking handsome in your fine uniforms. Dressing up and doing the terrible, terrible things you do. It makes me ashamed. But I blame myself, Ralf, not you.'

'Children, upstairs now!' said Mother, clapping her hands together, and this time they had no choice but to stand up and obey her.

But rather than going straight to their rooms, they closed the door and sat at the top of the stairs, trying to hear what was being said by the grown-ups down below. However, Mother and Father's voices were muffled and hard to make out, Grandfather's was not to be heard at all, while Grandmother's was surprisingly slurred. Finally, after a few minutes, the door slammed open and Gretel and Bruno darted back up the stairs while Grandmother retrieved her coat from the rack in the hallway.

'Ashamed!' she called out before she left. 'That a son of mine should be—'

'A patriot,' cried Father, who perhaps had never learned the rule about not interrupting your mother.

'A patriot indeed!' she cried out. 'The people you have to dinner in this house. Why, it makes me sick. And to see you in that uniform makes me want to tear the eyes from my head!' she added before storming out of the house and slamming the door behind her.

Bruno hadn't seen much of Grandmother after that and hadn't even had a chance to say goodbye to her before they moved to Out-With, but he missed her very much and decided to write her a letter.

That day he sat down with a pen and paper and told her how unhappy he was there and how much he wished he was back home in Berlin. He told her about the house and the garden and the bench with the plaque on it and the tall fence and the wooden telegraph poles and the barbed-wire bales and the hard ground beyond them and the huts and the small buildings and the smoke stacks and the soldiers, but mostly he told her about the people living there and their striped pyjamas and cloth caps, and then he told her how much he missed her and he signed off his letter 'your loving grandson, Bruno'.

Chapter Nine

Bruno Remembers That He Used to Enjoy Exploration

Nothing changed for quite a while at Out-With.

Bruno still had to put up with Gretel being less than friendly to him whenever she was in a bad mood, which was more often than not because she was a Hopeless Case.

And he still wished that he could go back home to Berlin, although the memories of that place were beginning to fade and, while he did mean to, it had been several weeks since he had even thought about sending another letter to Grandfather or Grandmother, let alone actually sitting down and writing one.

The soldiers still came and went every day of the week, holding meetings in Father's office, which was still Out Of Bounds At All Times And No Exceptions. Lieutenant Kotler still strode around in his black boots as if there was no one in the whole world of any more importance than him, and when he wasn't with Father he was standing in the drive-way talking to Gretel while she laughed hysterically and twirled her hair around her fingers, or whisper-ing alone in rooms with Mother.

The servants still came and washed things and swept things and cooked things and cleaned things and served things and took things away and kept their mouths shut unless they were spoken to. Maria still spent most of her time tidying things away and making sure that any item of clothing not currently being worn by Bruno was neatly folded in his wardrobe. And Pavel still arrived at the house every afternoon to peel the potatoes and the carrots and then put his white jacket on and serve at the dinner table. (From time to time Bruno saw him throw a glance in the direction of his knee, where a tiny scar from his swing-related accident was in evidence, but other than that they never spoke to each other.)

But then things changed. Father decided it was time for the children to return to their studies, and although it seemed ridiculous to Bruno that school should take place when there were only two students to teach, both Mother and Father agreed that a tutor should come to the house every day and fill their mornings and afternoons with lessons. A few morn-ings later a man called Herr Liszt rattled up the driveway on his boneshaker and it was time for school again. Herr Liszt was a mystery to Bruno.

Although he was friendly enough most of the time, never raising his hand to him like his old teacher in Berlin had done, something in his eyes made Bruno feel there was an anger inside him just waiting to get out.

Herr Liszt was particularly fond of history and geography, while Bruno preferred reading and art.

'Those things are useless to you,' insisted the teacher. 'A sound understanding of the social sciences is far more important in this day and age.'

'Grandmother always let us perform in plays back in Berlin,' Bruno pointed out.

'Your grandmother was not your teacher though, was she?' asked Herr Liszt. 'She was your grandmother. And here I am your teacher, so you will study the things that I say are important and not just the things you like yourself.'

'But aren't books important?' asked Bruno.

'Books about things that matter in the world, of course,' explained Herr Liszt. 'But not storybooks. Not books about things that never happened. How much do you know of your history anyway, young man?' (To his credit, Herr Liszt referred to Bruno as 'young man', like Pavel and unlike Lieutenant Kotler.)

'Well, I know I was born on April the fifteenth nineteen thirty-four—' said Bruno.

'Not *your* history,' interrupted Herr Liszt. 'Not

your own personal history. I mean the history of who you are, where you come from. Your family's heritage. The Fatherland.'

Bruno frowned and considered it. He wasn't entirely sure that Father had any land, because although the house in Berlin was a large and comfortable house, there wasn't very much garden space around it. And he was old enough to know that Out-With did not belong to them, despite all the land there. 'Not very much,' he admitted finally. 'Although I know quite a bit about the Middle Ages. I like stories about knights and adventures and exploring.'

Herr Liszt made a hissing sound through his teeth and shook his head angrily. 'Then this is what I am here to change,' he said in a sinister voice. 'To get your head out of your storybooks and teach you more about where you come from. About the great wrongs that have been done to you.'

Bruno nodded and felt quite pleased by this as he assumed that he would finally be given an explanation for why they had all been forced to leave their comfortable home and come to this terrible place, which must have been the greatest wrong ever committed to him in his short life.

Sitting alone in his room a few days later, Bruno started thinking about all the things he liked to do at home that he hadn't been able to do since he had come to Out-With. Most of them came about because he no longer had any friends to play with, and it wasn't as if Gretel would ever play with him. But there was one thing that he was able to do on his own and that he had done all the time back in Berlin, and that was exploring.

'When I was a child,' Bruno said to himself, 'I used to enjoy exploring. And that was in Berlin, where I knew everywhere and could find anything I wanted with a blindfold on. I've never really done any exploring here. Perhaps it's time to start.'

And then, before he could change his mind, Bruno jumped off his bed and rummaged in his wardrobe for an overcoat and an old pair of boots – the kind of clothes he thought a real explorer might wear – and prepared to leave the house.

There was no point doing any exploring inside. After all, this wasn't like the house in Berlin, which he could just about remember had hundreds of nooks and crannies, and strange little rooms, not to mention five floors if you counted the basement and the little room at the top with the window he needed to stand on tiptoes to see through. No, this was a terrible house for exploration. If there was any to be done it would have to be done outside.

For months now Bruno had been looking out of his bedroom window at the garden and the bench with the plaque on it, the tall fence and the wooden telegraph poles and all the other things he had written to Grandmother about in his most recent letter. And as often as he had watched the people, all the different kinds of people in their striped pyjamas, it had never really occurred to him to wonder what it was all about.

It was as if it were another city entirely, the people all living and working together side by side with the house where he lived. And were they really so different? All the people in the camp wore the same clothes, those pyjamas and their striped cloth caps too; and all the people who wandered through his house (with the exception of Mother, Gretel and him) wore uniforms of varying quality and decoration and caps and helmets with bright red-and-black armbands and carried guns and always looked terribly stern, as if it was all very important really and no one should think otherwise.

What exactly was the difference? he wondered to himself. And who decided which people wore the striped pyjamas and which people wore the uniforms?

Of course sometimes the two groups mixed. He'd often seen the people from his side of the fence on the other side of the fence, and when he watched it was clear that they were in charge. The pyjama people all jumped to attention whenever the soldiers approached and sometimes they fell to the ground and sometimes they didn't even get up and had to be carried away instead.

It's funny that I've never wondered about those people, Bruno thought. And it's funny that when you think of all the times the soldiers go over there – and he had even seen Father go over there on many occasions – that none of them had ever been invited back to the house.

Sometimes – not very often, but sometimes – a few of the soldiers stayed to dinner, and when they did a lot of frothy drinks were served and the moment Gretel and Bruno had put the last forkful of food in their mouths they were sent away to their rooms and then there was a lot of noise downstairs and some terrible singing too. Father and Mother obviously enjoyed the company of the soldiers – Bruno could tell that. But they'd never once invited any of the striped pyjama people to dinner.

Leaving the house, Bruno went round the back and looked up towards his own bedroom window which, from down here, did not look quite so high any more. You could probably jump out of it and not do too much damage to yourself, he considered, although he couldn't imagine the circumstances in which he would try such an idiotic thing. Perhaps if the house were on fire and he was trapped in there, but even then it would seem risky.

He looked as far to his right as he could see, and

the tall fence seemed to carry on in the sunlight and he was glad that it did because it meant that he didn't know what was up ahead and he could walk and find out and that was what exploration was all about after all. (There was one good thing that Herr Liszt had taught him about in their history lessons: men like Christopher Columbus and Amerigo Vespucci; men with such adventurous stories and interesting lives that it only confirmed in Bruno's mind that he wanted to be like them when he grew up.)

Before heading off in that direction, though, there was one final thing to investigate and that was the bench. All these months he'd been looking at it and staring at the plaque from a distance and calling it 'the bench with the plaque', but he still had no idea what it said. Looking left and right to make sure that no one was coming, he ran over to it and squinted as he read the words. It was only a small bronze plaque and Bruno read it quietly to himself.

'*Presented on the occasion of the opening of . . .*' He hesitated. '*Out-With Camp,*' he continued, stumbling over the name as usual. '*June nineteen forty.*'

He reached out and touched it for a moment, and the bronze was very cold so he pulled his fingers away before taking a deep breath and beginning his journey. The one thing Bruno tried not to think about was that he had been told on countless occasions by both Mother and Father that he was not allowed to walk in this direction, that he was not allowed anywhere near the fence or the camp, and most particularly that exploration was banned at Out-With.

With No Exceptions.

Chapter Ten

The Dot That Became a Speck That Became a Blob That Became a Figure That Became a Boy

The walk along the fence took Bruno a lot longer than he expected; it seemed to stretch on and on for several miles. He walked and walked, and when he looked back the house that he was living in became smaller and smaller until it vanished from sight altogether. During all this time he never saw anyone anywhere close to the fence; nor did he find any doors to let him inside, and he started to despair that his exploration was going to be entirely unsuccessful. In fact although the fence continued as far as the eye could see, the huts and buildings and smoke stacks were disappearing in the distance behind him and the fence seemed to be separating him from nothing but open space.

After walking for the best part of an hour and starting to feel a little hungry, he thought that maybe that was enough exploration for one day and it would be a good idea to turn back. However, just at that moment a small dot appeared in the distance and he narrowed his eyes to try to see what it was. Bruno remembered a book he had read in which a man was lost in the desert and because he hadn't had any food or water for several days had started to imagine that he saw wonderful restaurants and enormous fountains, but when he tried to eat or drink from them they disappeared into nothingness, just handfuls of sand. He wondered whether that was what was happening to him now.

But while he was thinking this his feet were taking him, step by step, closer and closer to the dot in the distance, which in the meantime had become a speck, and then began to show every sign of turning into a blob. And shortly after that the blob became a figure. And then, as Bruno got even closer, he saw that the thing was neither a dot nor a speck nor a blob nor a figure, but a person.

In fact it was a boy.

Bruno had read enough books about explorers to know that one could never be sure what one was going to find. Most of the time they came across something interesting that was just sitting there, minding its own business, waiting to be discovered (such as America). Other times they discovered something that was probably best left alone (like a dead mouse at the back of a cupboard).

The boy belonged to the first category. He was just

sitting there, minding his own business, waiting to be discovered.

Bruno slowed down when he saw the dot that became a speck that became a blob that became a figure that became a boy. Although there was a fence separating them, he knew that you could never be too careful with strangers and it was always best to approach them with caution. So he continued to walk, and before long they were facing each other.

'Hello,' said Bruno.

'Hello,' said the boy.

The boy was smaller than Bruno and was sitting on the ground with a forlorn expression. He wore the same striped pyjamas that all the other people on that side of the fence wore, and a striped cloth cap on his head. He wasn't wearing any shoes or socks and his feet were rather dirty. On his arm he wore an armband with a star on it.

When Bruno first approached the boy, he was sitting cross-legged on the ground, staring at the dust beneath him. However, after a moment he looked up and Bruno saw his face. It was quite a strange face too. His skin was almost the colour of grey, but not quite like any grey that Bruno had ever seen before. He had very large eyes and they were the colour of

caramel sweets; the whites were very white, and
when the boy looked at him all Bruno could see was
an enormous pair of sad eyes staring back.

Bruno was sure that he had never seen a skinnier
or sadder boy in his life but decided that he had
better talk to him.

'I've been exploring,' he said.

'Have you?' said the little boy.

'Yes. For almost two hours now.'

This was not strictly speaking true. Bruno had
been exploring for just over an hour but he didn't
think that exaggerating slightly would be too bad a
thing to do. It wasn't quite the same thing as lying
and made him seem more adventurous than he really
was.

'Have you found anything?' asked the boy.

'Very little.'

'Nothing at all?'

'Well, I found you,' said Bruno after a moment.

He stared at the boy and considered asking him
why he looked so sad but hesitated because he
thought it might sound rude. He knew that sometimes people who were sad didn't want to be asked
about it; sometimes they'd offer the information
themselves and sometimes they wouldn't stop talking
about it for months on end, but on this occasion
Bruno thought that he should wait before saying
anything. He had discovered something during his

exploration, and now that he was finally talking to one of the people on the other side of the fence it seemed like a good idea to make the most of the opportunity.

He sat down on the ground on his side of the fence and crossed his legs like the little boy and wished that he had brought some chocolate with him or perhaps a pastry that they could share.

'I live in the house on this side of the fence,' said Bruno.

'Do you? I saw the house once, from a distance, but I didn't see you.'

'My room is on the first floor,' said Bruno. 'I can see right over the fence from there. I'm Bruno, by the way.'

'I'm Shmuel,' said the little boy.

Bruno scrunched up his face, not sure that he had heard the little boy right. 'What did you say your name was?' he asked.

'Shmuel,' said the little boy as if it was the most natural thing in the world. 'What did you say *your* name was?'

'Bruno,' said Bruno.

'I've never heard of that name,' said Shmuel.

'And I've never heard of your name,' said Bruno. 'Shmuel.' He thought about it. 'Shmuel,' he repeated. 'I like the way it sounds when I say it. Shmuel. It sounds like the wind blowing.'

'Bruno,' said Shmuel, nodding his head happily. 'Yes, I think I like your name too. It sounds like someone who's rubbing their arms to keep warm.'

'I've never met anyone called Shmuel before,' said Bruno.

'There are dozens of Shmuels on this side of the fence,' said the little boy. 'Hundreds probably. I wish I had a name all of my own.'

'I've never met anyone called Bruno,' said Bruno. 'Other than me, of course. I think I might be the only one.'

'Then you're lucky,' said Shmuel.

'I suppose I am. How old are you?' he asked.

Shmuel thought about it and looked down at his fingers and they wiggled in the air, as if he was trying to calculate. 'I'm nine,' he said. 'My birthday is April the fifteenth nineteen thirty-four.'

Bruno stared at him in surprise. 'What did you say?' he asked.

'I said my birthday is April the fifteenth nineteen thirty-four.'

Bruno's eyes opened wide and his mouth made the shape of an O. 'I don't believe it,' he said.

'Why not?' asked Shmuel.

'No,' said Bruno, shaking his head quickly. 'I don't mean I don't believe *you*. I mean I'm surprised, that's all. Because *my* birthday is April the fifteenth too.

And *I* was born in nineteen thirty-four. We were born on the same day.'

Shmuel thought about this. 'So you're nine too,' he said.

'Yes. Isn't that strange?'

'Very strange,' said Shmuel. 'Because there may be dozens of Shmuels on this side of the fence but I don't think that I've ever met anyone with the same birthday as me before.'

'We're like twins,' said Bruno.

'A little bit,' agreed Shmuel.

Bruno felt very happy all of a sudden. A picture came into his head of Karl and Daniel and Martin, his three best friends for life, and he remembered how much fun they used to have together back in Berlin and he realized how lonely he had been at Out-With.

'Do you have many friends?' asked Bruno, cocking his head a little to the side as he waited for an answer.

'Oh yes,' said Shmuel. 'Well, sort of.'

Bruno frowned. He had hoped that Shmuel might have said no as it would give them something else in common. '*Close* friends?' he asked.

'Well, not very close,' said Shmuel. 'But there are a lot of us – boys our age, I mean – on this side of the fence. We fight a lot of the time though. That's why I come out here. To be on my own.'

'It's so unfair,' said Bruno. 'I don't see why I have to be stuck over here on this side of the fence where there's no one to talk to and no one to play with and you get to have dozens of friends and are probably playing for hours every day. I'll have to speak to Father about it.'

'Where did you come from?' asked Shmuel, narrowing his eyes and looking at Bruno curiously.

'Berlin.'

'Where's that?'

Bruno opened his mouth to answer but found that he wasn't entirely sure. 'It's in Germany, of course,' he said. 'Don't you come from Germany?'

'No, I'm from Poland,' said Shmuel.

Bruno frowned. 'Then why do you speak German?' he asked.

'Because you said hello in German. So I answered in German. Can you speak Polish?'

'No,' said Bruno, laughing nervously. 'I don't know anyone who can speak two languages. And especially no one of our age.'

'Mama is a teacher in my school and she taught me German,' explained Shmuel. 'She speaks French too. And Italian. And English. She's very clever. I don't speak French or Italian yet, but she said she'd teach me English one day because I might need to know it.'

'Poland,' said Bruno thoughtfully, weighing up the

word on his tongue. 'That's not as good as Germany, is it?'

Shmuel frowned. 'Why isn't it?' he asked.

'Well, because Germany is the greatest of all countries,' Bruno replied, remembering something that he had overheard Father discussing with Grandfather on any number of occasions. 'We're superior.'

Shmuel stared at him but didn't say anything, and Bruno felt a strong desire to change the subject because even as he had said the words, they didn't sound quite right to him and the last thing he wanted was for Shmuel to think that he was being unkind.

'Where is Poland anyway?' he asked after a few silent moments had passed.

'Well, it's in Europe,' said Shmuel.

Bruno tried to remember the countries he had been taught about in his most recent geography class with Herr Liszt. 'Have you ever heard of Denmark?' he asked.

'No,' said Shmuel.

'I think Poland is in Denmark,' said Bruno, growing more confused even though he was trying to sound clever. 'Because *that's* many miles away,' he repeated for added confirmation.

Shmuel stared at him for a moment and opened his mouth and closed it twice, as if he was considering his words carefully. 'But this is Poland,' he said finally.

'Is it?' asked Bruno.

'Yes it is. And Denmark's quite far away from both Poland and Germany.'

Bruno frowned. He'd heard of all these places but he always found it hard to get them straight in his head. 'Well, yes,' he said. 'But it's all relative, isn't it? Distance, I mean.' He wished they could get off the subject as he was starting to think he was entirely wrong and made a private resolution to pay more attention in future in geography class.

'I've never been to Berlin,' said Shmuel.

'And I don't think I'd ever been to Poland before I came here,' said Bruno, which was true because he hadn't. 'That is, if this really *is* Poland.'

'I'm sure it is,' said Shmuel quietly. 'Although it's not a very nice part of it.'

'No.'

'Where I come from is a lot nicer.'

'It's certainly not as nice as Berlin,' said Bruno. 'In Berlin we had a big house with five floors if you counted the basement and the little room at the top with the window. And there were lovely streets and shops and fruit and vegetable stalls and any number of cafés. But if you ever go there I wouldn't recommend walking around town on a Saturday afternoon because there are far too many people there then and you get pushed from pillar to post. And it was much nicer before things changed.'

'How do you mean?' asked Shmuel.

'Well, it used to be very quiet there,' explained Bruno, who didn't like to talk about how things had changed. 'And I was able to read in bed at night. But now it's quite noisy sometimes, and scary, and we have to turn all the lights off when it starts to get dark.'

'Where I come from is much nicer than Berlin,' said Shmuel, who had never been to Berlin. 'Everyone there is very friendly and we have lots of people in our family and the food is a lot better too.'

'Well, we'll have to agree to disagree,' said Bruno, who didn't want to fight with his new friend.

'All right,' said Shmuel.

'Do you like exploring?' asked Bruno after a moment.

'I've never really done any,' admitted Shmuel.

'I'm going to be an explorer when I grow up,' said Bruno, nodding his head quickly. 'At the moment I can't do very much more than read about explorers, but at least that means that when I'm one myself, I won't make the mistakes they did.'

Shmuel frowned. 'What kind of mistakes?' he asked.

'Oh, countless ones,' explained Bruno. 'The thing about exploring is that you have to know whether the thing you've found is worth finding. Some things are just sitting there, minding their own business, waiting to be discovered. Like America. And other things are probably better off left alone. Like a dead mouse at the back of a cupboard.'

'I think I belong to the first category,' said Shmuel.

'Yes,' replied Bruno. 'I think you do. Can I ask you something?' he added after a moment.

'Yes,' said Shmuel.

Bruno thought about it. He wanted to phrase the question just right.

'Why are there so many people on that side of the fence?' he asked. 'And what are you all doing there?'

Chapter Eleven

The Fury

Some months earlier, just after Father received the new uniform which meant that everyone had to call him 'Commandant' and just before Bruno came home to find Maria packing up his things, Father came home one evening in a state of great excitement, which was terribly unlike him, and marched into the living room where Mother, Bruno and Gretel were sitting reading their books.

'Thursday night,' he announced. 'If we've any plans for Thursday night we have to cancel them.'

'You can change your plans if you want to,' said Mother, 'but I've made arrangements to go to the theatre with—'

'The Fury has something he wants to discuss with me,' said Father, who was allowed to interrupt Mother even if no one else was. 'I just got a phone call this afternoon. The only time he can make it is Thursday evening and he's invited himself to dinner.'

Mother's eyes opened wide and her mouth made

the shape of an O. Bruno stared at her and wondered whether this was what he looked like when he was surprised about something.

'But you're not serious,' said Mother, growing a little pale. 'He's coming here? To our house?'

Father nodded. 'At seven o'clock,' he said. 'So we'd better think about something special for dinner.'

'Oh my,' said Mother, her eyes moving back and forth quickly as she started to think of all the things that needed doing.

'Who's the Fury?' asked Bruno.

'You're pronouncing it wrong,' said Father, pronouncing it correctly for him.

'The Fury,' said Bruno again, trying to get it right but failing again.

'No,' said Father, 'the— Oh, never mind!'

'Well, who is he anyway?' asked Bruno again.

Father stared at him, astonished. 'You know perfectly well who the Fury is,' he said.

'I don't,' said Bruno.

'He runs the country, idiot,' said Gretel, showing off as sisters tend to do. (It was things like this that made her such a Hopeless Case.) 'Don't you ever read a newspaper?'

'Don't call your brother an idiot, please,' said Mother.

'Can I call him stupid?'

'I'd rather you didn't.'

Gretel sat down again, disappointed, but stuck her tongue out at Bruno nonetheless.

'Is he coming alone?' asked Mother.

'I forgot to ask,' said Father. 'But I presume he'll be bringing *her* with him.'

'Oh my,' said Mother again, standing up and counting in her head the number of things she had to organize before Thursday, which was only two evenings away. The house would have to be cleaned from top to bottom, the windows washed, the dining-room table stained and varnished, the food ordered, the maid's and butler's uniforms washed and pressed, and the crockery and glasses polished until they sparkled.

Somehow, despite the fact that the list seemed to grow longer and longer all the time, Mother managed to get everything finished on time, although she commented over and over again that the evening would be a greater success if some people helped out a little bit more around the house.

An hour before the Fury was due to arrive Gretel and Bruno were brought downstairs, where they received a rare invitation into Father's office. Gretel was wearing a white dress and knee socks and her hair had been twisted into corkscrew curls. Bruno was wearing a pair of dark brown shorts, a plain white shirt and a dark brown tie. He had a new pair of shoes for the occasion and was very proud of them, even though they were too small for him and were pinching his feet and making it difficult for him to walk. All these preparations and fine clothes seemed a little extravagant, all the same, because Bruno and Gretel weren't even invited to dinner; they had eaten an hour earlier.

'Now, children,' said Father, sitting behind his desk and looking from his son to his daughter and back again as they stood before him. 'You know that there is a very special evening ahead of us, don't you?'

They nodded.

'And that it is very important for my career that tonight goes well.'

They nodded again.

'Then there are a number of ground rules which need to be set down before we begin.' Father was a big believer in ground rules. Whenever there was a special or important occasion in the house, more of them were created.

'Number one,' said Father. 'When the Fury arrives you will stand in the hall quietly and prepare to greet him. You do not speak until he speaks to you and then you reply in a clear tone, enunciating each word precisely. Is that understood?'

'Yes, Father,' mumbled Bruno.

'That's exactly the type of thing we don't want,'

said Father, referring to the mumbling. 'You open your mouth and speak like an adult. The last thing we need is for either of you to start behaving like children. If the Fury ignores you then you do not say anything either, but look directly ahead and show him the respect and courtesy that such a great leader deserves.'

'Of course, Father,' said Gretel in a very clear voice.

'And when Mother and I are at dinner with the Fury, you are both to remain in your rooms very quietly. There is to be no running around, no sliding down banisters' – and here he looked very deliberately at Bruno – 'and no interrupting us. Is that understood? I don't want either of you causing chaos.'

Bruno and Gretel nodded and Father stood up to indicate that this meeting was at an end.

'Then the ground rules are established,' he said.

Three quarters of an hour later the doorbell rang and the house erupted in excitement. Bruno and Gretel took their places standing side by side by the staircase and Mother waited beside them, wringing her hands together nervously. Father gave them all a quick glance and nodded, looking pleased by what he saw, and then opened the door.

Two people stood outside: a rather small man and a taller woman.

Father saluted them and ushered them inside, where Maria, her head bowed even lower than usual, took their coats and the introductions were made. They spoke to Mother first, which gave Bruno an opportunity to stare at their guests and decide for himself whether they deserved all the fuss being made of them.

The Fury was far shorter than Father and not, Bruno supposed, quite as strong. He had dark hair, which was cut quite short, and a tiny moustache – so tiny in fact that Bruno wondered why he bothered with it at all or whether he had simply forgotten a piece when he was shaving. The woman standing beside him, however, was quite the most beautiful woman he had ever seen in his life. She had blonde hair and very red lips, and while the Fury spoke to Mother she turned and looked at Bruno and smiled, making him go red with embarrassment.

'And these are my children, Fury,' said Father as Gretel and Bruno stepped forward. 'Gretel and Bruno.'

'And which is which?' the Fury said, which made everyone laugh except for Bruno, who thought it was perfectly obvious which was which and hardly cause for a joke. The Fury stretched out his hand and shook theirs and Gretel gave a careful, rehearsed curtsy. Bruno was delighted when it went wrong and she almost fell over.

'What charming children,' said the beautiful blonde woman. 'And how old are they, might I ask?'

'I'm twelve but he's only nine,' said Gretel, looking at her brother with disdain. 'And I can speak French too,' she added, which was not strictly speaking true, although she had learned a few phrases in school.

'Yes, but why would you want to?' asked the Fury, and this time no one laughed; instead they shifted uncomfortably from foot to foot and Gretel stared at him, unsure whether he wanted an answer or not.

The matter was resolved quickly, however, as the Fury, who was the rudest guest Bruno had ever witnessed, turned round and walked directly into the dining room and promptly sat down at the head of the table – in Father's seat! – without another word. A little flustered, Mother and Father followed him inside and Mother gave instructions to Lars that he could start heating up the soup.

'I can speak French too,' said the beautiful blonde woman, leaning down and smiling at the two children. She didn't seem to be as frightened of the Fury as Mother and Father were. 'French is a beautiful language and you are very clever to be learning it.'

'Eva,' shouted the Fury from the other room, clicking his fingers as if she were some sort of puppy dog. The woman rolled her eyes and stood up slowly and turned round.

'I like your shoes, Bruno, but they look a little tight on you,' she added with a smile. 'If they are, you should tell your mother, before they cause you to injure yourself.'

'They are a *little* tight,' admitted Bruno.

'I don't normally wear my hair in curls,' said Gretel, jealous of the attention that her brother was getting.

'But why not?' asked the woman. 'It's so pretty that way.'

'Eva!' roared the Fury for a second time, and now she started to walk away from them.

'It was lovely to meet you both,' she said, before stepping into the dining room and sitting down on the Fury's left-hand side. Gretel walked towards the stairs but Bruno stayed rooted to the ground, watching the blonde woman until she caught his eye again and waved at him, just as Father appeared and closed the doors with a jerk of his head – from which Bruno understood that it was time to go to his room, to sit quietly, and not to make any noise and certainly not to slide down any banisters.

The Fury and Eva stayed for the best part of two hours and neither Gretel nor Bruno were invited downstairs to say goodbye to them. Bruno watched them leave from his bedroom window and noticed that when they stepped towards their car, which he was impressed to see had a chauffeur, the Fury did not open the door for his companion but instead climbed in and started reading a newspaper, while she said goodbye once again to Mother and thanked her for the lovely dinner.

What a horrible man, thought Bruno.

Later that night Bruno overheard snippets of Mother and Father's conversation. Certain phrases drifted through the keyhole or under the door of Father's office and up the staircase and round the landing and under the door of Bruno's bedroom. Their voices were unusually loud and Bruno could only make out a few fragments of them:

'. . . to leave Berlin. And for such a place . . .' Mother was saying.

'. . . no choice, at least not if we want to continue . . .' said Father.

'. . . as if it's the most natural thing in the world and it's not, it's just not . . .' said Mother.

'. . . what would happen is I would be taken away and treated like a . . .' said Father.

'. . . expect them to grow up in a place like . . .' said Mother.

'. . . and that's an end to the matter. I don't want to hear another word on the subject . . .' said Father.

That must have been the end of the conversation because Mother left Father's office then and Bruno fell asleep.

A couple of days later he came home from school

to find Maria standing in his bedroom, pulling all his belongings out of the wardrobe and packing them in four large wooden crates, even the things he'd hidden at the back that belonged to him and were nobody else's business, and that is where the story began.

Chapter Twelve

Shmuel Thinks of an Answer to Bruno's Question

'All I know is this,' began Shmuel. 'Before we came here I lived with my mother and father and my brother Josef in a small flat above the store where Papa makes his watches. Every morning we ate our breakfast together at seven o'clock and while we went to school, Papa mended the watches that people brought to him and made new ones too. I had a beautiful watch that he gave me but I don't have it any more. It had a golden face and I wound it up every night before I went to sleep and it always told the right time.'

'What happened to it?' asked Bruno.

'They took it from me,' said Shmuel.

'Who?'

'The soldiers, of course,' said Shmuel as if this was the most obvious thing in the world.

'And then one day things started to change,' he continued. 'I came home from school and my mother was making armbands for us from a special cloth and drawing a star on each one. Like this.' Using his finger he drew a design in the dusty ground beneath him.

'And every time we left the house, she told us we had to wear one of these armbands.'

'My father wears one too,' said Bruno. 'On his uniform. It's very nice. It's bright red with a black-and-white design on it.' Using his finger he drew another design in the dusty ground on his side of the fence.

'Yes, but they're different, aren't they?' said Shmuel.

'No one's ever given me an armband,' said Bruno.

'But I never asked to wear one,' said Shmuel.

'All the same,' said Bruno, 'I think I'd quite like one. I don't know which one I'd prefer though, your one or Father's.'

Shmuel shook his head and continued with his story. He didn't often think about these things any more because remembering his old life above the watch shop made him very sad.

'We wore the armbands for a few months,' he said.

'And then things changed again. I came home one day and Mama said we couldn't live in our house any more—'

'That happened to me too!' shouted Bruno, delighted that he wasn't the only boy who'd been forced to move. 'The Fury came for dinner, you see, and the next thing I knew we moved here. And I *hate* it here,' he added in a loud voice. 'Did he come to your house and do the same thing?'

'No, but when we were told we couldn't live in our house we had to move to a different part of Cracow, where the soldiers built a big wall and my mother and father and my brother and I all had to live in one room.'

'All of you?' asked Bruno. 'In one room?'

'And not just us,' said Shmuel. 'There was another family there and the mother and father were always fighting with each other and one of the sons was bigger than me and he hit me even when I did nothing wrong.'

'You can't have all lived in the one room,' said Bruno, shaking his head. 'That doesn't make any sense.'

'All of us,' said Shmuel, nodding his head. 'Eleven in total.'

Bruno opened his mouth to contradict him again – he didn't really believe that eleven people could live in the same room together – but changed his mind.

'We lived there for some more months,' continued Shmuel, 'all of us in that one room. There was one small window in it but I didn't like to look out of it because then I would see the wall and I hated the wall because our real home was on the other side of it. And this part of town was the bad part because it was always noisy and it was impossible to sleep. And I hated Luka, who was the boy who kept hitting me even when I did nothing wrong.'

'Gretel hits me sometimes,' said Bruno. 'She's my sister,' he added. 'And a Hopeless Case. But soon I'll be bigger and stronger than she is and she won't know what's hit her then.'

'Then one day the soldiers all came with huge trucks,' continued Shmuel, who didn't seem all that interested in Gretel. 'And everyone was told to leave the houses. Lots of people didn't want to and they hid wherever they could find a place but in the end I think they caught everyone. And the trucks took us to a train and the train . . .' He hesitated for a moment and bit his lip. Bruno thought he was going to start crying and couldn't understand why.

'The train was horrible,' said Shmuel. 'There were too many of us in the carriages for one thing. And there was no air to breathe. And it smelled awful.'

'That's because you all crowded onto one train,' said Bruno, remembering the two trains he had seen at the station when he left Berlin. 'When we came here, there was another one on the other side of the platform but no one seemed to see it. That was the one we got. You should have got on it too.'

'I don't think we would have been allowed,' said Shmuel, shaking his head. 'We weren't able to get out of our carriage.'

'The doors are at the end,' explained Bruno.

'There weren't any doors,' said Shmuel.

'Of course there were doors,' said Bruno with a sigh. 'They're at the end,' he repeated. 'Just past the buffet section.'

'There weren't any doors,' insisted Shmuel. 'If there had been, we would all have got off.'

Bruno mumbled something under his breath along the lines of 'Of course there were', but he didn't say it very loud so Shmuel didn't hear.

'When the train finally stopped,' continued Shmuel, 'we were in a very cold place and we all had to walk here.'

'We had a car,' said Bruno, out loud now.

'And Mama was taken away from us, and Papa and Josef and I were put into the huts over there and that's where we've been ever since.'

Shmuel looked very sad when he told this story and Bruno didn't know why; it didn't seem like such a terrible thing to him, and after all much the same thing had happened to him.

'Are there many other boys over there?' asked Bruno.

'Hundreds,' said Shmuel.

Bruno's eyes opened wide. 'Hundreds?' he said, amazed. 'That's not fair at all. There's no one to play with on this side of the fence. Not a single person.'

'We don't play,' said Shmuel.

'Don't play? Why ever not?'

'What would we play?' he asked, his face looking confused at the idea of it.

'Well, I don't know,' said Bruno. 'All sorts of things. Football, for example. Or exploration. What's the exploration like over there anyway? Any good?'

Shmuel shook his head and didn't answer. He looked back towards the huts and turned back to Bruno then. He didn't want to ask the next question but the pains in his stomach made him.

'You don't have any food on you, do you?' he asked.

'Afraid not,' said Bruno. 'I meant to bring some chocolate but I forgot.'

'Chocolate,' said Shmuel very slowly, his tongue moving out from behind his teeth. 'I've only ever had chocolate once.'

'Only once? I love chocolate. I can't get enough of it although Mother says it'll rot my teeth.'

'You don't have any bread, do you?'

Bruno shook his head. 'Nothing at all,' he said.

'Dinner isn't served until half past six. What time do you have yours?'

Shmuel shrugged his shoulders and pulled himself to his feet. 'I think I'd better get back,' he said.

'Perhaps you can come to dinner with us one evening,' said Bruno, although he wasn't sure it was a very good idea.

'Perhaps,' said Shmuel, although he didn't sound convinced.

'Or I could come to you,' said Bruno. 'Perhaps I could come and meet your friends,' he added hopefully. He had hoped that Shmuel would suggest this. himself but there didn't seem to be any sign of that.

'You're on the wrong side of the fence though,' said Shmuel.

'I could crawl under,' said Bruno, reaching down and lifting the wire off the ground. In the centre, between the wooden telegraph poles, it lifted quite easily and a boy as small as Bruno could easily fit through.

Shmuel watched him do this and backed away nervously. 'I have to go back,' he said.

'Some other afternoon then,' said Bruno.

'I'm not supposed to be here. If they catch me I'll be in trouble.'

He turned and walked away and Bruno noticed again just how small and skinny his new friend was. He didn't say anything about this because he knew only too well how unpleasant it was being criticized for something as silly as your height, and the last thing he wanted to do was be unkind to Shmuel.

'I'll come back tomorrow,' shouted Bruno to the departing boy and Shmuel said nothing in reply; in fact he started to run off back to the camp, leaving Bruno all on his own.

Bruno decided that that was more than enough exploration for one day and he set off home, excited about what had happened and wanting nothing more than to tell Mother and Father and Gretel – who would be so jealous that she might just explode – and Maria and Cook and Lars all about his adventure that afternoon and his new friend with the funny name and the fact that they had the same birthday, but the closer he got to his own house, the more he started to think that that might not be a good idea.

After all, he reasoned, they might not want me to be friends with him any more and if that happens they might stop me coming out here at all. By the time he went through his front door and smelled the beef that was roasting in the oven for dinner he had decided that it was better to keep the whole story to himself for the moment and not breathe a word about it. It would be his own secret. Well, his and Shmuel's.

Bruno was of the opinion that when it came to parents, and especially when it came to sisters, what they didn't know couldn't hurt them.

Chapter Thirteen

The Bottle of Wine

As week followed week it started to become clear to Bruno that he would not be going home to Berlin in the foreseeable future and that he could forget about sliding down the banisters in his comfortable home or seeing Karl or Daniel or Martin any time soon.

However, with each day that passed he began to get used to being at Out-With and stopped feeling quite so unhappy about his new life. After all, it wasn't as if he had nobody to talk to any more. Every afternoon when classes were finished Bruno took the long walk along the fence and sat and talked with his new friend Shmuel until it was time to come home, and that had started to make up for all the times he had missed Berlin.

One afternoon, as he was filling his pockets with some bread and cheese from the kitchen fridge to take with him, Maria came in and stopped when she saw what he was doing.

'Hello,' said Bruno, trying to appear as casual as

possible. 'You gave me a fright. I didn't hear you coming.'

'You're not eating again, surely?' asked Maria with a smile. 'You had lunch, didn't you? And you're still hungry?'

'A little,' said Bruno. 'I'm going for a walk and thought I might get peckish on the way.'

Maria shrugged her shoulders and went over to the cooker, where she put a pan of water on to boil. Laid out on the surface beside it was a pile of potatoes and carrots, ready for peeling when Pavel arrived later in the afternoon. Bruno was about to leave when the food caught his eye and a question came into his mind that had been bothering him for some time. He hadn't been able to think of anyone to ask before, but this seemed like a perfect moment and the perfect person.

'Maria,' he said, 'can I ask you a question?'

The maid turned round and looked at him in surprise. 'Of course, Master Bruno,' she said.

'And if I ask you this question, will you promise not to tell anyone that I asked it?'

She narrowed her eyes suspiciously but nodded. 'All right,' she said. 'What is it you want to know?'

'It's about Pavel,' said Bruno. 'You know him, don't you? The man who comes and peels the vegetables and then waits on us at table.'

'Oh yes,' said Maria with a smile. She sounded

relieved that his question wasn't going to be about anything more serious. 'I know Pavel. We've spoken on many occasions. Why do you ask about him?'

'Well,' said Bruno, choosing his words quite carefully in case he said something he shouldn't, 'do you remember soon after we got here when I made the swing on the oak tree and fell and cut my knee?'

'Yes,' said Maria. 'It's not hurting you again, is it?'

'No, it's not that,' said Bruno. 'But when I hurt it, Pavel was the only grown-up around and he brought me in here and cleaned it and washed it and put the green ointment on it, which stung but I suppose it made it better, and then he put a bandage on it.'

'That's what anyone would do if someone's hurt,' said Maria.

'I know,' he continued. 'Only he told me then that he wasn't really a waiter at all.'

Maria's face froze a little and she didn't say anything for a moment. Instead she looked away and licked her lips a little before nodding her head. 'I see,' she said. 'And what did he say he was really?'

'He said he was a doctor,' said Bruno. 'Which didn't seem right at all. He's not a doctor, is he?'

'No,' said Maria, shaking her head. 'No, he's not a doctor. He's a waiter.'

'I knew it,' said Bruno, feeling very pleased with himself. 'Why did he lie to me then? It doesn't make any sense.'

'Pavel is not a doctor any more, Bruno,' said Maria quietly. 'But he was. In another life. Before he came here.'

Bruno frowned and thought about it. 'I don't understand,' he said.

'Few of us do,' said Maria.

'But if he was a doctor, why isn't he one still?'

Maria sighed and looked out of the window to make sure that no one was coming, then nodded towards the chairs and both she and Bruno sat down.

'If I tell you what Pavel told me about his life,' she said, 'you mustn't tell anyone – do you understand? We would all get in terrible trouble.'

'I won't tell anyone,' said Bruno, who loved to hear secrets and almost never spread them around, except when it was totally necessary of course, and there was nothing he could do about it.

'All right,' said Maria. 'This is as much as I know.'

Bruno was late arriving at the place in the fence where he met Shmuel every day, but as usual his new friend was sitting cross-legged on the ground waiting for him.

'I'm sorry I'm late,' he said, handing some of the bread and cheese through the wire – the bits that he hadn't already eaten on the way when he had grown a little peckish after all. 'I was talking to Maria.'

'Who's Maria?' asked Shmuel, not looking up as he gobbled down the food hungrily.

'She's our maid,' explained Bruno. 'She's very nice although Father says she's overpaid. But she was telling me about this man Pavel who chops our vegetables for us and waits on table. I think he lives on your side of the fence.'

Shmuel looked up for a moment and stopped eating. 'On my side?' he asked.

'Yes. Do you know him? He's very old and has a white jacket that he wears when he's serving dinner. You've probably seen him.'

'No,' said Shmuel, shaking his head. 'I don't know him.'

'But you must,' said Bruno irritably, as if Shmuel were being deliberately difficult. 'He's not as tall as some adults and he has grey hair and stoops over a little.'

'I don't think you realize just how many people live on this side of the fence,' said Shmuel. 'There are thousands of us.'

'But this one's name is Pavel,' insisted Bruno. 'When I fell off my swing he cleaned out the cut so it didn't get infected and put a bandage on my leg. Anyway, the reason I wanted to tell you about him is because he's from Poland too. Like you.'

'Most of us here are from Poland,' said Shmuel.

'Although there are some from other places too, like Czechoslovakia and—'

'Yes, but that's why I thought you might know him. Anyway, he was a doctor in his home town before he came here but he's not allowed to be a doctor any more and if Father had known that he had cleaned my knee when I hurt myself then there would have been trouble.'

'The soldiers don't normally like people getting better,' said Shmuel, swallowing the last piece of bread. 'It usually works the other way round.'

Bruno nodded, even though he didn't quite know what Shmuel meant, and gazed up into the sky. After a few moments he looked through the wire and asked another question that had been preying on his mind.

'Do you know what you want to be when you grow up?' he asked.

'Yes,' said Shmuel. 'I want to work in a zoo.'

'A zoo?' asked Bruno.

'I like animals,' said Shmuel quietly.

'I'm going to be a soldier,' said Bruno in a determined voice. 'Like Father.'

'I wouldn't like to be a soldier,' said Shmuel.

'I don't mean one like Lieutenant Kotler,' said Bruno quickly. 'Not one who strides around as if he owns the place and laughs with your sister and whispers with your mother. I don't think he's a good soldier at all. I mean one like Father. One of the good soldiers.'

'There aren't any good soldiers,' said Shmuel.

'Of course there are,' said Bruno.

'Who?'

'Well, Father, for one,' said Bruno. 'That's why he has such an impressive uniform and why everyone calls him Commandant and does whatever he says. The Fury has big things in mind for him because he's such a good soldier.'

'There aren't any good soldiers,' repeated Shmuel.

'Except Father,' repeated Bruno, who was hoping that Shmuel wouldn't say that again because he didn't want to have to argue with him. After all, he was the only friend he had here at Out-With. But Father was Father, and Bruno didn't think it was right for someone to say something bad about him.

Both boys stayed very quiet for a few minutes, neither one wanting to say anything he might regret.

'You don't know what it's like here,' said Shmuel eventually in a low voice, his words barely carrying across to Bruno.

'You don't have any sisters, do you?' asked Bruno quickly, pretending he hadn't heard that because then he wouldn't have to answer.

'No,' said Shmuel, shaking his head.

'You're lucky,' said Bruno. 'Gretel's only twelve and she thinks she knows everything but she's a

Hopeless Case really. She sits looking out of her window and when she sees Lieutenant Kotler coming she runs downstairs into the hallway and pretends that she was there all along. The other day I caught her doing it and when he came in she jumped and said, *Why, Lieutenant Kotler, I didn't know you were here*, and I know for a fact that she was waiting for him.'

Bruno hadn't been looking at Shmuel as he said all that, but when he looked again he noticed that his friend had grown even more pale than usual.

'What's wrong?' he asked. 'You look as if you're about to be sick.'

'I don't like talking about him,' said Shmuel.

'About who?' asked Bruno.

'Lieutenant Kotler. He scares me.'

'He scares me too a little,' admitted Bruno. 'He's a bully. And he smells funny. It's all that cologne he puts on.' And then Shmuel started to shiver slightly and Bruno looked around, as if he could see rather than feel whether it was cold or not. 'What's the matter?' he asked. 'It's not that cold, is it? You should have brought a jumper, you know. The evenings *are* getting chillier.'

Later that evening Bruno was disappointed to find that Lieutenant Kotler was joining him, Mother, Father and Gretel for dinner. Pavel was wearing his white jacket as usual and served them as they ate.

Bruno watched Pavel as he went around the table and found that he felt sad whenever he looked at him. He wondered whether the white jacket he wore as a waiter was the same as the white jacket he had worn before as a doctor. As he brought the plates in and set them down in front of each of them, and while they ate their food and talked, he stepped back towards the wall and held himself perfectly still, neither looking ahead nor not. It was as if his body had gone to sleep standing up and with his eyes open.

Whenever anyone needed anything, Pavel would bring it immediately, but the more Bruno watched him the more he was sure that catastrophe was going to strike. He seemed to grow smaller and smaller each week, if such a thing were possible, and the colour that should have been in his cheeks had drained almost entirely away. His eyes appeared heavy with tears and Bruno thought that one good blink might bring on a torrent.

When Pavel came in with the plates, Bruno couldn't help but notice that his hands were shaking slightly under the weight of them. And when he stepped back to his usual position he seemed to sway on his feet and had to press a hand against the wall to steady himself. Mother had to ask twice for her extra helping of soup before he heard her, and he let the bottle of wine empty without having opened another one in time to fill Father's glass.

'Herr Liszt won't let us read poetry or plays,' complained Bruno during the main course. As they had company for dinner, the family were dressed formally – Father in his uniform, Mother in a green dress that set off her eyes, and Gretel and Bruno in the clothes they wore to church when they lived in Berlin. 'I asked him if we could read them just one day a week but he said no, not while he was in charge of our education.'

'I'm sure he has his reasons,' said Father, attacking a leg of lamb.

'All he wants us to do is study history and geography,' said Bruno. 'And I'm starting to hate history and geography.'

'Don't say hate, Bruno, please,' said Mother.

'Why do you hate history?' asked Father, laying down his fork for a moment and looking across the table at his son, who shrugged his shoulders, a bad habit of his.

'Because it's boring,' he said.

'Boring?' said Father. 'A son of mine calling the study of history boring? Let me tell you this, Bruno,' he went on, leaning forward and pointing his knife at the boy, 'it's history that's got us here today. If it wasn't for history, none of us would be sitting around this table now. We'd be safely back at our table in our house in Berlin. We are correcting history here.'

'It's still boring,' repeated Bruno, who wasn't really paying attention.

'You'll have to forgive my brother, Lieutenant Kotler,' said Gretel, laying a hand on his arm for a moment, which made Mother stare at her and narrow her eyes. 'He's a very ignorant little boy.'

'I am not ignorant,' snapped Bruno, who had had enough of her insults. 'You'll have to forgive my sister, Lieutenant Kotler,' he added politely, 'but she's a Hopeless Case. There's very little we can do for her. The doctors say she's gone past the point of help.'

'Shut up,' said Gretel, blushing scarlet.

'You shut up,' said Bruno with a broad smile.

'Children, please,' said Mother.

Father tapped his knife on the table and everyone was silent. Bruno glanced in his direction. He didn't look angry exactly, but he did look as if he wasn't going to put up with much more arguing.

'I enjoyed history very much when I was a boy,' said Lieutenant Kotler after a few silent moments. 'And although my father was a professor of literature at the university, I preferred the social sciences to the arts.'

'I didn't know that, Kurt,' said Mother, turning to look at him for a moment. 'Does he still teach then?'

'I suppose so,' said Lieutenant Kotler. 'I don't really know.'

'Well, how could you not know?' she asked, frowning at him. 'Don't you keep in touch with him?'

The young lieutenant chewed on a mouthful of lamb and it gave him an opportunity to think of a reply. He looked to Bruno as if he regretted having brought the matter up in the first place.

'Kurt,' repeated Mother, 'don't you keep in touch with your father?'

'Not really,' he replied, shrugging his shoulders dismissively and not turning his head to look at her. 'He left Germany some years ago. Nineteen thirty-eight, I think it was. I haven't seen him since then.'

Father stopped eating for a moment and stared across at Lieutenant Kotler, frowning slightly. 'And where did he go?' he asked.

'I beg your pardon, Herr Commandant?' asked Lieutenant Kotler, even though Father had spoken in a perfectly clear voice.

'I asked you where he went,' he repeated. 'Your father. The professor of literature. Where did he go when he left Germany?'

Lieutenant Kotler's face grew a little red and he stuttered somewhat as he spoke. 'I believe ... I believe he is currently in Switzerland,' he said finally. 'The last I heard he was teaching at a university in Berne.'

'Oh, but Switzerland's a beautiful country,' said

Mother quickly. 'I haven't ever been there, I admit, but from what I hear—'

'He can't be very old, your father,' said Father, his deep voice silencing them all. 'I mean you're only . . . what? Seventeen? Eighteen years old?'

'I've just turned nineteen, Herr Commandant.'

'So your father would be . . . in his forties, I expect?'

Lieutenant Kotler said nothing but continued to eat although he didn't appear to be enjoying his food at all.

'Strange that he chose not to stay in the Fatherland,' said Father.

'We're not close, my father and I,' said Lieutenant Kotler quickly, looking around the table as if he owed everyone an explanation. 'Really, we haven't spoken in years.'

'And what reason did he give, might I ask,' continued Father, 'for leaving Germany at the moment of her greatest glory and her most vital need, when it is incumbent upon all of us to play our part in the national revival? Was he tubercular?'

Lieutenant Kotler stared at Father, confused. 'I beg your pardon?' he asked.

'Did he go to Switzerland to take the air?' explained Father. 'Or did he have a particular reason for leaving Germany? In nineteen thirty-eight,' he added after a moment.

'I'm afraid I don't know, Herr Commandant,' said Lieutenant Kotler. 'You would have to ask him.'

'Well, that would be rather difficult to do, wouldn't it? With him being so far away, I mean. But perhaps that was it. Perhaps he was ill.' Father hesitated before picking up his knife and fork again and continuing to eat. 'Or perhaps he had ... disagreements.'

'Disagreements, Herr Commandant?'

'With government policy. One hears tales of men like this from time to time. Curious fellows, I imagine. Disturbed, some of them. Traitors, others. Cowards too. Of course you have informed your superiors of your father's views, Lieutenant Kotler?'

The young lieutenant opened his mouth and then swallowed, despite the fact that he hadn't been eating anything.

'Never mind,' said Father cheerfully. 'Perhaps it is not an appropriate subject of conversation for the dinner table. We can discuss it in more depth at a later time.'

'Herr Commandant,' said Lieutenant Kotler, leaning forward anxiously, 'I can assure you—'

'It is *not* an appropriate subject of conversation for the dinner table,' repeated Father sharply, silencing him immediately, and Bruno looked from one to the other, both enjoying and being frightened by the atmosphere at the same time.

'I'd love to go to Switzerland,' said Gretel after a lengthy silence.

'Eat your dinner, Gretel,' said Mother.

'But I was just saying!'

'Eat your dinner,' Mother repeated and was about to say more but she was interrupted by Father calling for Pavel again.

'What's the matter with you tonight?' he asked as Pavel uncorked the new bottle. 'This is the fourth time I've had to ask for more wine.'

Bruno watched him, hoping he was feeling all right, although he managed to release the cork without any accidents. But after he had filled Father's glass and turned to refill Lieutenant Kotler's, he lost his grip of the bottle somehow and it fell crashing, glug-glug-glugging its contents out directly onto the young man's lap.

What happened then was both unexpected and extremely unpleasant. Lieutenant Kotler grew very angry with Pavel and no one – not Bruno, not Gretel, not Mother and not even Father – stepped in to stop him doing what he did next, even though none of them could watch. Even though it made Bruno cry and Gretel grow pale.

Later that night, when Bruno went to bed, he thought about all that had happened over dinner. He remembered how kind Pavel had been to him on the afternoon he had made the swing, and how he had stopped his knee from bleeding and been very gentle in the way he administered the green ointment. And while Bruno realized that Father was generally a very kind and thoughtful man, it hardly seemed fair or right that no one had stopped Lieutenant Kotler getting so angry at Pavel, and if that was the kind of thing that went on at Out-With then he'd better not disagree with anyone any more about anything; in fact he would do well to keep his mouth shut and cause no chaos at all. Some people might not like it.

His old life in Berlin seemed like a very distant memory now and he could hardly even remember what Karl, Daniel or Martin looked like, except for the fact that one of them was a ginger.

Chapter Fourteen

Bruno Tells a Perfectly Reasonable Lie

For several weeks after this Bruno continued to leave the house when Herr Liszt had gone home for the day and Mother was having one of her afternoon naps, and made the long trek along the fence to meet Shmuel, who almost every afternoon was waiting there for him, sitting cross-legged on the ground, staring at the dust beneath him.

One afternoon Shmuel had a black eye, and when Bruno asked him about it he just shook his head and said that he didn't want to talk about it. Bruno assumed that there were bullies all over the world, not just in schools in Berlin, and that one of them had done this to Shmuel. He felt an urge to help his friend but he couldn't think of anything he could do to make it better, and he could tell that Shmuel wanted to pretend it had never happened.

Every day Bruno asked Shmuel whether he would be allowed to crawl underneath the wire so that they could play together on the other side of the fence, but every day Shmuel said no, it wasn't a good idea.

'I don't know why you're so anxious to come across here anyway,' said Shmuel. 'It's not very nice.'

'You haven't tried living in my house,' said Bruno. 'For one thing it doesn't have five floors, only three. How can anyone live in so small a space as that?' He'd forgotten Shmuel's story about the eleven people all living in the same room together before they had come to Out-With, including the boy Luka who kept hitting him even when he did nothing wrong.

One day Bruno asked why Shmuel and all the other people on that side of the fence wore the same striped pyjamas and cloth caps.

'That's what they gave us when we got here,' explained Shmuel. 'They took away our other clothes.'

'But don't you ever wake up in the morning and feel like wearing something different? There must be something else in your wardrobe.'

Shmuel blinked and opened his mouth to say something but then thought better of it.

'I don't even like stripes,' said Bruno, although this wasn't actually true. In fact he did like stripes and he felt increasingly fed up that he had to wear trousers and shirts and ties and shoes that were too tight for him when Shmuel and his friends got to wear striped pyjamas all day long.

A few days later Bruno woke up and for the first time in weeks it was raining heavily. It had started at some point during the night and Bruno even thought that it might have woken him up, but it was hard to tell because once he was awake there was no way of knowing how that had happened. As he ate his breakfast that morning, the rain continued. Through all the morning classes with Herr Liszt, the rain continued. While he ate his lunch, the rain continued. And while they finished another session of history and geography in the afternoon, the rain continued. This was bad news for it meant that he wouldn't be able to leave the house and meet Shmuel.

That afternoon Bruno lay on his bed with a book but found it hard to concentrate, and just then the Hopeless Case came in to see him. She didn't often come to Bruno's room, preferring to arrange and rearrange her collection of dolls constantly during her free time. However, something about the wet weather had put her off her game and she couldn't face playing it again just yet.

'What do you want?' asked Bruno.

'That's a nice welcome,' said Gretel.

'I'm reading,' said Bruno.

'What are you reading?' she asked him, and rather than answer he simply turned the cover towards her so she could see for herself.

She made a raspberry sound through her lips and

some of her spit landed on Bruno's face. 'Boring,' she said in a sing-song voice.

'It's not boring at all,' said Bruno. 'It's an adventure. It's better than dolls, that's for sure.'

Gretel didn't rise to the bait on that one. 'What are you doing?' she repeated, irritating Bruno even further.

'I told you, I'm trying to read,' he said in a grumpy voice. 'If some people would just let me.'

'I've got nothing to do,' she replied. 'I hate the rain.'

Bruno found this hard to understand. It wasn't as if she ever did anything anyway, unlike him, who had adventures and explored places and had made a friend. She very rarely left the house at all. It was as if she had decided to be bored simply because on this occasion she didn't have a choice about staying inside. But still, there are moments when a brother and sister can lay down their instruments of torture for a moment and speak as civilized human beings and Bruno decided to make this one of those moments.

'I hate the rain too,' he said. 'I should be with Shmuel by now. He'll think I've forgotten him.'

The words were out of his mouth quicker than he could stop them and he felt a pain in his stomach and grew furious with himself for saying that.

'You should be with who?' asked Gretel.

'What's that?' asked Bruno, blinking back at her.

'Who did you say you should be with?' she asked again.

'I'm sorry,' said Bruno, trying to think quickly. 'I didn't quite hear you. Could you say that again?'

'*Who did you say you should be with?*' she shouted, leaning forward so there could be no mistake this time.

'I never said I should be with anyone,' he said.

'Yes, you did. You said that someone will think you've forgotten them.'

'Pardon?'

'Bruno!' she said in a threatening voice.

'Are you mad?' he asked, trying to make her think that she had entirely made it up, only he wasn't very convincing for he wasn't a natural actor like Grandmother, and Gretel shook her head and pointed a finger at him.

'What did you say, Bruno?' she insisted. 'You said there was someone you should be with. Who was it? Tell me! There's no one around here to play with, is there?'

Bruno considered the dilemma he was in. On the one hand his sister and he had one crucial thing in common: they weren't grown-ups. And although he had never bothered to ask her, there was every chance that she was just as lonely as he was at Out-With. After all, back in Berlin she had had Hilda and

Isobel and Louise to play with; they may have been annoying girls but at least they were her friends. Here she had no one at all except her collection of lifeless dolls. Who knew how mad Gretel was after all? Perhaps she thought the dolls were talking to her.

But at the same time there was the undeniable fact that Shmuel was *his* friend and not hers and he didn't want to share him. There was only one thing for it and that was to lie.

'I have a new friend,' he began. 'A new friend that I go to see every day. And he'll be waiting for me now. But you can't tell anyone.'

'Why not?'

'Because he's an imaginary friend,' said Bruno, trying his best to look embarrassed, just like Lieutenant Kotler had when he had become trapped in his story about his father in Switzerland. 'We play together every day.'

Gretel opened her mouth and stared at him before breaking into a laugh. 'An imaginary friend!' she cried. 'Aren't you a little old for an imaginary friend?'

Bruno tried to look ashamed and embarrassed in order to make his story more convincing. He squirmed on the bed and didn't look her in the eye, which worked a treat and made him think that perhaps he wasn't such a bad actor after all. He wished that he could make himself go red, but it was difficult to do that so he thought of embarrassing things that had happened to him over the years and wondered whether these would do the trick.

He thought of the time he had forgotten to lock the bathroom door and Grandmother had walked in and seen everything. He thought of the time he had put his hand up in class and called the teacher 'Mother' and everyone had laughed at him. He thought of the time he'd fallen off his bicycle in front of a group of girls when he was trying to do a special trick and cut his knee and cried.

One of them worked and his face started to go red.

'Look at you,' said Gretel, confirming it. 'You've gone all red.'

'Because I didn't want to tell you,' said Bruno.

'An imaginary friend. Honestly, Bruno, you're a hopeless case.'

Bruno smiled because he knew two things. The first was that he had got away with his lie and the second was that if anyone was the Hopeless Case around here, it wasn't him.

'Leave me alone,' he said. 'I want to read my book.'

'Well, why don't you lie down and close your eyes and let your imaginary friend read it to you?' said Gretel, delighted with herself now because she had something on him and she wasn't going to let it drop in a hurry. 'Save you a job.'

'Maybe I should send him to throw all your dolls out of your window,' he said.

'You do and there'll be trouble,' said Gretel, and he knew that she meant it. 'Well, tell me this, Bruno. What do you and this imaginary friend of yours do together that makes him so special?'

Bruno thought about it. He realized that he actually wanted to talk about Shmuel a little bit and that this might be a way to do it without having to tell her the truth about his existence.

'We talk about everything,' he told her. 'I tell him about our house back in Berlin and all the other houses and the streets and the fruit and vegetable stalls and the cafés, and how you shouldn't go into town on a Saturday afternoon unless you want to get pushed from pillar to post, and about Karl and Daniel and Martin and how they were my three best friends for life.'

'How interesting,' said Gretel sarcastically because she had recently had a birthday and turned thirteen and thought that sarcasm was the very height of sophistication. 'And what does he tell you?'

'He tells me about his family and the watch shop that he used to live over and the adventures he had coming here and the friends he used to have and the people he knows here and about the boys who he used to play with but he doesn't any more because they disappeared without even saying goodbye to him.'

'He sounds like a barrel of laughs,' said Gretel. 'I wish he was *my* imaginary friend.'

'And yesterday he told me that his grandfather hasn't been seen for days and no one knows where he is and whenever he asks his father about him he starts crying and hugs him so hard that he's worried he's going to squeeze him to death.'

Bruno got to the end of his sentence and realized that his voice had gone very quiet. These were things that Shmuel *had* told him, but for some reason he hadn't really understood at the time how sad that must have made his friend. When Bruno said them out loud himself he felt terrible that he hadn't tried to say anything to cheer Shmuel up and instead had started talking about something silly, like exploring. *I'll say sorry for that tomorrow*, he told himself.

'If Father knew you were talking to imaginary friends, you'd be in for it,' said Gretel. 'I think you should stop.'

'Why?' asked Bruno.

'Because it's not healthy,' she said. 'It's the first sign of madness.'

Bruno nodded. 'I don't think I can stop,' he said after a very long pause. 'I don't think I want to.'

'Well, all the same,' said Gretel, who was becoming friendlier and friendlier by the second, 'I'd keep it to myself if I were you.'

'Well,' said Bruno, trying to look sad, 'you're

probably right. You won't tell anyone, will you?'

She shook her head. 'No one. Except my own imaginary friend.'

Bruno gasped. 'Do you have one?' he asked, picturing her at another part of the fence, talking to a girl her own age, the two of them being sarcastic together for hours at a time.

'No,' she said, laughing. 'I'm thirteen years old, for heaven's sake! I can't afford to act like a child even if you can.'

And with that she flounced out of the room, and Bruno could hear her talking to her dolls in the room across the hall and scolding them for getting themselves into such a mess while her back was turned that she had no choice but to rearrange them and did they think she had nothing better to do with her time?

'Some people!' she said loudly, before getting down to work.

Bruno tried to return to his book, but he'd lost interest in it for now and stared out at the rain instead and wondered whether Shmuel, wherever he was, was thinking about him too and missing their conversations as much as he was.

Chapter Fifteen

Something He Shouldn't Have Done

For several weeks the rain was on and off and on and off and Bruno and Shmuel did not see as much of each other as they would have liked. When they did meet Bruno found that he was starting to worry about his friend because he seemed to be getting even thinner by the day and his face was growing more and more grey. Sometimes he brought more bread and cheese with him to give to Shmuel, and from time to time he even managed to hide a piece of chocolate cake in his pocket, but the walk from the house to the place in the fence where the two boys met was a long one and sometimes Bruno got hungry on the way and found that one bite of the cake would lead to another, and that in turn led to another, and by the time there was only one mouthful left he knew it would be wrong to give that to Shmuel because it would only tease his appetite and not satisfy it.

Father's birthday was coming up soon, and

although he said he didn't want a fuss, Mother arranged a party for all the officers serving at Out-With and a great fuss was made to prepare for it. Every time she sat down to make more plans for the party, Lieutenant Kotler was there beside her to help, and between them they seemed to make more lists than could ever possibly be needed.

Bruno decided to make a list of his own. A list of all the reasons why he didn't like Lieutenant Kotler.

There was the fact that he never smiled and always looked as if he was trying to find somebody to cut out of his will.

On the rare occasions when he spoke to Bruno, he addressed him as 'little man', which was just plain nasty because, as Mother pointed out, he just hadn't had his growth spurt yet.

Not to mention the fact that he was always in the living room with Mother and making jokes with her, and Mother laughed at his jokes more than she laughed at Father's.

Once when Bruno was watching the camp from his bedroom window he saw a dog approach the fence and start barking loudly, and when Lieutenant Kotler heard it he marched right over to the dog and shot it. Then there was all that nonsense that Gretel came out with whenever he was around.

And Bruno still hadn't forgotten the evening with Pavel, the waiter who was really a doctor, and how angry the young lieutenant had been.

Also, whenever Father was called away to Berlin on an overnight trip the lieutenant hung around the house as if he were in charge: he would be there when Bruno was going to bed and be back again in the morning before he even woke up.

There were a lot more reasons why Bruno didn't like Lieutenant Kotler, but these were the first things that came into his mind.

On the afternoon before the birthday party Bruno was in his room with the door open when he heard Lieutenant Kotler arriving at the house and speaking to someone, although he couldn't hear anyone answering back. A few minutes later, as he was coming downstairs, he heard Mother giving instructions about what needed to be done and Lieutenant Kotler saying, 'Don't worry, this one knows which side his bread is buttered on,' and then laughing in a nasty way.

Bruno walked towards the living room with a new book Father had given him called *Treasure Island*, intending to sit in there for an hour or two while he read it, but as he walked through the hallway he ran into Lieutenant Kotler, who was just leaving the kitchen.

'Hello, little man,' the soldier said, sneering at him as usual.

'Hello,' said Bruno, frowning.

'What are you up to then?'

Bruno stared at him and started thinking of seven more reasons to dislike him. 'I'm going in there to read my book,' he said, pointing towards the living room.

Without a word Kotler whipped the book out of Bruno's hands and started to flick through it. '*Treasure Island*,' he said. 'What's it about then?'

'Well, there's an island,' said Bruno slowly, to make sure that the soldier could keep up. 'And there's treasure on it.'

'I could have guessed that,' said Kotler, looking at him as if there were things he would do to the boy if he were a son of his and not the son of the Commandant. 'Tell me something I don't know about it.'

'There's a pirate in it,' said Bruno. 'Called Long John Silver. And a boy called Jim Hawkins.'

'An English boy?' asked Kotler.

'Yes,' said Bruno.

'Grunt,' grunted Kotler.

Bruno stared at him and wondered how long it would be before he gave back his book. He didn't seem particularly interested in it, but when Bruno reached for it he pulled it away.

'Sorry,' he said, holding it out again, and when Bruno reached for it he pulled it away for the second time. 'Oh, I'm so sorry,' he repeated and held it out once more, and this time Bruno swiped it out of his hand quicker than he could pull it away.

'Aren't you quick,' muttered Lieutenant Kotler between his teeth.

Bruno tried to step past him, but for some reason Lieutenant Kotler seemed to want to talk to him today.

'All set for the party, are we?' he asked.

'Well, *I* am,' said Bruno, who had been spending more time with Gretel lately and had developed a liking for sarcasm. 'I can't speak for you.'

'There'll be a lot of people here,' said Lieutenant Kotler, breathing in heavily and looking around as if this were his house and not Bruno's. 'We'll be on your best behaviour, won't we?'

'Well, *I'll* be,' said Bruno. 'I can't speak for you.'

'You've a lot to say for such a little man,' said Lieutenant Kotler.

Bruno narrowed his eyes and wished he were taller, stronger and eight years older. A ball of anger exploded inside him and made him wish that he had the courage to say exactly what he wanted to say. It was one thing, he decided, to be told what to do by Mother and Father – that was perfectly reasonable and to be expected – but it was another thing entirely to be told what to do by someone else. Even by someone with a fancy title like 'Lieutenant'.

'Oh, Kurt, precious, you're still here,' said Mother,

stepping out of the kitchen and coming towards them. 'I have a little free time now if— Oh!' she said, noticing Bruno standing there. 'Bruno! What are you doing here?'

'I was going into the living room to read my book,' said Bruno. 'Or I was trying to at least.'

'Well, run along into the kitchen for the moment,' she said. 'I need a private word with Lieutenant Kotler.'

And they stepped into the living room together as Lieutenant Kotler closed the doors in Bruno's face.

Seething with anger, Bruno went into the kitchen and got the biggest surprise of his life. There, sitting at the table, a long way from the other side of the fence, was Shmuel. Bruno could barely believe his eyes.

'Shmuel!' he said. 'What are you doing here?'

Shmuel looked up and his terrified face broke into a broad smile when he saw his friend standing there. 'Bruno!' he said.

'What are you doing here?' repeated Bruno, for although he still didn't quite understand what took place on the other side of the fence, there was something about the people from there that made him think they shouldn't be here in his house.

'He brought me,' said Shmuel.

'He?' asked Bruno. 'You don't mean Lieutenant Kotler?'

'Yes. He said there was a job for me to do here.'

And when Bruno looked down he saw sixty-four small glasses, the ones Mother used when she was having one of her medicinal sherries, sitting on the kitchen table, and beside them a bowl of warm soapy water and lots of paper napkins.

'What on earth are you doing?' asked Bruno.

'They asked me to polish the glasses,' said Shmuel. 'They said they needed someone with tiny fingers.'

As if to prove something that Bruno already knew, he held his hand out and Bruno couldn't help but notice that it was like the hand of the pretend skeleton that Herr Liszt had brought with him one day when they were studying human anatomy.

'I'd never noticed before,' he said in a disbelieving voice, almost to himself.

'Never noticed what?' asked Shmuel.

In reply, Bruno held his own hand out so that the tips of their middle fingers were almost touching. 'Our hands,' he said. 'They're so different. Look!'

The two boys looked down at the same time and the difference was easy to see. Although Bruno was small for his age, and certainly not fat, his hand appeared healthy and full of life. The veins weren't visible through the skin, the fingers weren't little more than dying twigs. Shmuel's hand, however, told a very different story.

'How did it get like that?' he asked.

'I don't know,' said Shmuel. 'It used to look more like yours, but I didn't notice it changing. Everyone on my side of the fence looks like this now.'

Bruno frowned. He thought about the people in their striped pyjamas and wondered what was going on at Out-With and whether it wasn't a very bad idea if it made people look so unhealthy. None of it made any sense to him. Not wanting to look at Shmuel's hand any longer, Bruno turned round and opened the refrigerator, rooting about inside it for something to eat. There was half a stuffed chicken left over from lunch time, and Bruno's eyes sparkled in delight for there were very few things in life that he enjoyed more than cold chicken with sage and onion stuffing. He took a knife from the drawer and cut himself a few healthy slices and coated them with the stuffing before turning back to his friend.

'I'm very glad you're here,' he said, speaking with his mouth full. 'If only you didn't have to polish the glasses, I could show you my room.'

'He told me not to move from this seat or there'd be trouble.'

'I wouldn't mind him,' said Bruno, trying to sound braver than he really was. 'This isn't his house, it's mine, and when Father's away I'm in charge. Can you believe he's never even read *Treasure Island*?'

Shmuel looked as if he wasn't really listening; instead his eyes were focused on the slices of chicken and stuffing that Bruno was throwing casually into his mouth. After a moment Bruno realized what he was looking at and immediately felt guilty.

'I'm sorry, Shmuel,' he said quickly. 'I should have given you some chicken too. Are you hungry?'

'That's a question you never have to ask me,' said Shmuel who, although he had never met Gretel in his life, knew something about sarcasm too.

'Wait there, I'll cut some off for you,' said Bruno, opening the fridge and cutting another three healthy slices.

'No, if he comes back—' said Shmuel, shaking his head quickly and looking back and forth towards the door.

'If who comes back? You don't mean Lieutenant Kotler?'

'I'm just supposed to be cleaning the glasses,' he said, looking at the bowl of water in front of him in despair and then looking back at the slices of chicken that Bruno held out to him.

'He's not going to mind,' said Bruno, who was confused by how anxious Shmuel seemed. 'It's only food.'

'I can't,' said Shmuel, shaking his head and looking as if he was going to cry. 'He'll come back, I know he will,' he continued, his sentences running quickly together. 'I should have eaten them when you offered them, now it's too late, if I take them he'll come in and—'

'Shmuel! Here!' said Bruno, stepping forward and putting the slices in his friend's hand. 'Just eat them. There's lots left for our tea – you don't have to worry about that.'

The boy stared at the food in his hand for a moment and then looked up at Bruno with wide and grateful but terrified eyes. He threw one more glance in the direction of the door and then seemed to make a decision, because he thrust all three slices into his mouth in one go and gobbled them down in twenty seconds flat.

'Well, you don't have to eat them so quickly,' said Bruno. 'You'll make yourself sick.'

'I don't care,' said Shmuel, giving a faint smile. 'Thank you, Bruno.'

Bruno smiled back and he was about to offer him some more food, but just at that moment Lieutenant Kotler reappeared in the kitchen and stopped when he saw the two boys talking. Bruno stared at him, feeling the atmosphere grow heavy, sensing Shmuel's shoulders sinking down as he reached for another glass and began polishing. Ignoring Bruno, Lieutenant Kotler marched over to Shmuel and glared at him.

'What are you doing?' he shouted. 'Didn't I tell you to polish those glasses?'

Shmuel nodded his head quickly and started to tremble a little as he picked up another napkin and dipped it in the water.

'Who told you that you were allowed to talk in this house?' continued Kotler. 'Do you dare to disobey me?'

'No, sir,' said Shmuel quietly. 'I'm sorry, sir.'

He looked up at Lieutenant Kotler, who frowned, leaning forward slightly and tilting his head as he examined the boy's face. 'Have you been eating?' he asked him in a quiet voice, as if he could scarcely believe it himself.

Shmuel shook his head.

'You *have* been eating,' insisted Lieutenant Kotler. 'Did you steal something from that fridge?'

Shmuel opened his mouth and closed it. He opened it again and tried to find words, but there were none. He looked towards Bruno, his eyes pleading for help.

'Answer me!' shouted Lieutenant Kotler. 'Did you steal something from that fridge?'

'No, sir. He gave it to me,' said Shmuel, tears welling up in his eyes as he threw a sideways glance at Bruno. 'He's my friend,' he added.

'Your . . . ?' began Lieutenant Kotler, looking across at Bruno in confusion. He hesitated. 'What do you mean he's your friend?' he asked. 'Do you know this boy, Bruno?'

Bruno's mouth dropped open and he tried to remember the way you used your mouth if you wanted to say the word 'yes'. He'd never seen anyone look so terrified as Shmuel did at that moment and he wanted to say the right thing to make things better, but then he realized that he couldn't; because he was feeling just as terrified himself.

'Do you know this boy?' repeated Kotler in a louder voice. 'Have you been talking to the prisoners?'

'I . . . he was here when I came in,' said Bruno. 'He was cleaning glasses.'

'That's not what I asked you,' said Kotler. 'Have you seen him before? Have you talked to him? Why does he say you're his friend?'

Bruno wished he could run away. He hated Lieutenant Kotler, but he was advancing on him now and all Bruno could think of was the afternoon when he had seen him shooting a dog and the evening when Pavel had made him so angry that he—

'Tell me, Bruno!' shouted Kotler, his face growing red. 'I won't ask you a third time.'

'I've never spoken to him,' said Bruno immediately. 'I've never seen him before in my life. I don't know him.'

Lieutenant Kotler nodded and seemed satisfied with the answer. Very slowly he turned his head back to look at Shmuel, who wasn't crying any more, merely staring at the floor and looking as if he was trying to convince his soul not to live inside his tiny body any more, but to slip away and sail to the door and rise up into the sky, gliding through the clouds until it was very far away.

'You will finish polishing all these glasses,' said Lieutenant Kotler in a very quiet voice now, so quiet that Bruno almost couldn't hear him. It was as if all his anger had just changed into something else. Not quite the opposite, but something unexpected and dreadful. 'And then I will come to collect you and bring you back to the camp, where we will have a discussion about what happens to boys who steal. This is understood, yes?'

Shmuel nodded and picked up another napkin and started to polish another glass; Bruno watched as his fingers shook and knew that he was terrified of breaking one. His heart sank, but as much as he wanted to, he couldn't look away.

'Come on, little man,' said Lieutenant Kotler, coming towards Bruno now and putting an unfriendly arm around his shoulder. 'You go to the living room and read your book and leave this little — to finish his work.' He used the same word he had used to Pavel when he had sent him to find the tyre.

Bruno nodded and turned round and left the kitchen without looking back. His stomach churned inside him and he thought for a moment that he was going to be sick. He had never felt so ashamed in his life; he had never imagined that he could behave so cruelly. He wondered how a boy who thought he was a good person really could act in such a cowardly way towards a friend. He sat in the living room for several hours but couldn't concentrate on his book and didn't dare to go back to the kitchen until later that evening, when Lieutenant Kotler had already come back and collected Shmuel and taken him away again.

Every afternoon that followed, Bruno returned to the place in the fence where they met, but Shmuel was never there. After almost a week he was convinced that what he had done was so terrible that he would never be forgiven, but on the seventh day he was delighted to see that Shmuel was waiting for him, sitting cross-legged on the ground as usual and staring at the dust beneath him.

'Shmuel,' he said, running towards him and sitting down, almost crying with relief and regret. 'I'm so sorry, Shmuel. I don't know why I did it. Say you'll forgive me.'

'It's all right,' said Shmuel, looking up at him now. There was a lot of bruising on his face and Bruno grimaced, and for a moment he forgot about his apology.

'What happened to you?' he asked and then didn't wait for an answer. 'Was it your bicycle? Because that happened to me back in Berlin a couple of years ago. I fell off when I was going too fast and was black and blue for weeks. Does it hurt?'

'I don't feel it any more,' said Shmuel.

'It looks like it hurts.'

'I don't feel anything any more,' said Shmuel.

'Well, I am sorry about last week,' said Bruno. 'I hate that Lieutenant Kotler. He thinks he's in charge but he isn't.' He hesitated for a moment, not wanting to get sidetracked. He felt that he should say it one last time and really mean it. 'I'm very sorry, Shmuel,' he said in a clear voice. 'I can't believe I didn't tell him the truth. I've never let a friend down like that before. Shmuel, I'm ashamed of myself.'

And when he said that, Shmuel smiled and nodded and Bruno knew that he was forgiven, and then Shmuel did something that he had never done before. He lifted the bottom of the fence up like he did whenever Bruno brought him food, but this time he reached his hand out and held it there, waiting until Bruno did the same, and then the two boys shook hands and smiled at each other.

It was the first time they had ever touched.

Chapter Sixteen

The Haircut

It had been almost a year since Bruno had come home to find Maria packing his things, and his memories of life in Berlin had almost all faded away. When he thought back he could remember that Karl and Martin were two of his three best friends for life, but try as he might he couldn't remember who the other one was. And then something happened that meant that for two days he could leave Out-With and return to his old house: Grandmother had died and the family had to go home for the funeral.

While he was there, Bruno realized he wasn't quite as small as he had been when he left because he could see over things that he couldn't see over before, and when they stayed in their old house he could look through the window on the top floor and see across Berlin without having to stand on tiptoes.

Bruno hadn't seen his grandmother since leaving Berlin but he had thought about her every day. The things he remembered most about her were the productions that she and he and Gretel performed at Christmas and birthdays and how she always had the perfect costume to suit whatever role he played. When he thought that they would never be able to do that again it made him very sad indeed.

The two days they spent in Berlin were also very sad ones. There was the funeral, and Bruno and Gretel and Father and Mother and Grandfather sat in the front row, Father wearing his most impressive uniform, the starched and pressed one with the decorations. Father was particularly sad, Mother told Bruno, because he had fought with Grandmother and they hadn't made it up before she died.

There were a lot of wreaths delivered to the church and Father was proud of the fact that one of them had been sent by the Fury, but when Mother heard she said that Grandmother would turn in her grave if she knew it was there.

Bruno felt almost glad when they returned to Out-With. The house there had become his home now and he'd stopped worrying about the fact that it had only three floors rather than five, and it didn't bother him so much that the soldiers came and went as if they owned the place. It slowly dawned on him that things weren't too bad there after all, especially since he'd met Shmuel. He knew that there were many things he should be happy about, like the fact that Father and Mother seemed cheerful all the time now and Mother didn't have to take as many of her afternoon naps or medicinal sherries. And Gretel was going through a phase – Mother's words – and tended to keep out of his way.

There was also the fact that Lieutenant Kotler had been transferred away from Out-With and wasn't around to make Bruno feel angry and upset all the time. (His departure had come about very suddenly and there had been a lot of shouting between Father and Mother about it late at night, but he was gone, that was for sure, and he wasn't coming back; Gretel was inconsolable.) That was something else to be happy about: no one called him 'little man' any more.

But the best thing was that he had a friend called Shmuel.

He enjoyed walking along the fence every afternoon and was pleased to see that his friend seemed a lot happier these days and his eyes didn't seem so sunken, although his body was still ridiculously skinny and his face unpleasantly grey.

One day, while sitting opposite him at their usual place, Bruno remarked, 'This is the strangest friendship I've ever had.'

'Why?' asked Shmuel.

'Because every other boy I've ever been friends with has been someone that I've been able to play with,' he replied. 'And we never get to play together. All we get to do is sit here and talk.'

'I like sitting here and talking,' said Shmuel.

'Well, I do too of course,' said Bruno. 'But it's a pity we can't do something more exciting from time to time. A bit of exploring, perhaps. Or a game of football. We've never even seen each other without all this wire fencing in the way.'

Bruno often made comments like this because he wanted to pretend that the incident a few months earlier when he had denied his friendship with Shmuel had never taken place. It still preyed on his mind and made him feel bad about himself, although Shmuel, to his credit, seemed to have forgotten all about it.

'Maybe someday we will,' said Shmuel. 'If they ever let us out.'

Bruno started to think more and more about the two sides of the fence and the reason it was there in the first place. He considered speaking to Father or Mother about it but suspected that they would either be angry with him for mentioning it or tell him something unpleasant about Shmuel and his family, so instead he did something quite unusual. He decided to talk to the Hopeless Case.

Gretel's room had changed quite considerably since the last time he had been there. For one thing there wasn't a single doll in sight. One afternoon a month or so earlier, around the time that Lieutenant Kotler had left Out-With, Gretel had decided that she didn't like dolls any more and had put them all into four large bags and thrown them away. In their place she had hung up maps of Europe that Father had given her, and every day she put little pins into them and moved the pins around constantly after consulting the daily newspaper. Bruno thought she might be going mad. But still, she didn't tease him or bully him as much as she used to, so he thought there could be no harm in talking to her.

'Hello,' he said, knocking politely on her door because he knew how angry she always got if he just went in.

'What do you want?' asked Gretel, who was sitting at her dressing table, experimenting with her hair.

'Nothing,' said Bruno.

'Then go away.'

Bruno nodded but came inside anyway and sat down on the side of the bed. Gretel watched him from out of the side of her eyes but didn't say anything.

'Gretel,' he said finally, 'can I ask you something?'

'If you make it quick,' she said.

'Everything here at Out-With—' he began, but she interrupted him immediately.

'It's not called Out-With, Bruno,' she said angrily, as if this was the worst mistake anyone had ever made in the history of the world. 'Why can't you pronounce it right?'

'It *is* called Out-With,' he protested.

'It's not,' she insisted, pronouncing the name of the camp correctly for him.

Bruno frowned and shrugged his shoulders at the same time. 'But that's what I said,' he said.

'No it's not. Anyway, I'm not going to argue with you,' said Gretel, losing her patience already, for she had very little of it to begin with. 'What is it anyway? What do you want to know?'

'I want to know about the fence,' he said firmly, deciding that this was the most important thing to begin with. 'I want to know why it's there.'

Gretel turned round in her chair and looked at him curiously. 'You mean you don't know?' she asked.

'No,' said Bruno. 'I don't understand why we're not allowed on the other side of it. What's so wrong with us that we can't go over there and play?'

Gretel stared at him and then suddenly started laughing, only stopping when she saw that Bruno was being perfectly serious.

'Bruno,' she said in a childish voice, as if this was the most obvious thing in the world, 'the fence isn't there to stop us from going over there. It's to stop them from coming over here.'

Bruno considered this but it didn't make things any clearer. 'But why?' he asked.

'Because they have to be kept together,' explained Gretel.

'With their families, you mean?'

'Well, yes, with their families. But with their own kind too.'

'What do you mean, their own kind?'

Gretel sighed and shook her head. 'With the other Jews, Bruno. Didn't you know that? That's why they have to be kept together. They can't mix with us.'

'Jews,' said Bruno, testing the word out. He quite liked the way it sounded. 'Jews,' he repeated. 'All the people over that side of the fence are Jews.'

'Yes, that's right,' said Gretel.

'Are we Jews?'

Gretel opened her mouth wide, as if she had been slapped in the face. 'No, Bruno,' she said. 'No, we most certainly are not. And you shouldn't even say something like that.'

'But why not? What are we then?'

'We're . . .' began Gretel, but then she had to stop to think about it. 'We're . . .' she repeated, but she wasn't quite sure what the answer to this question really was. 'Well we're not Jews,' she said finally.

'I know we're not,' said Bruno in frustration. 'I'm asking you, if we're not Jews, what are we instead?'

'We're the opposite,' said Gretel, answering quickly and sounding a lot more satisfied with this answer. 'Yes, that's it. We're the opposite.'

'All right,' said Bruno, pleased that he had it settled in his head at last. 'And the Opposite live on this side of the fence and the Jews live on that.'

'That's right, Bruno.'

'Don't the Jews like the Opposite then?'

'No, it's us who don't like them, stupid.'

Bruno frowned. Gretel had been told time and time again that she wasn't allowed to call him stupid but still she persisted with it.

'Well, why don't we like them?' he asked.

'Because they're Jews,' said Gretel.

'I see. And the Opposite and the Jews don't get along.'

'No, Bruno,' said Gretel, but she said this slowly because she had discovered something unusual in her hair and was examining it carefully.

'Well, can't someone just get them together and—'

Bruno was interrupted by the sound of Gretel breaking into a piercing scream; one that woke Mother up from her afternoon nap and brought her running into the bedroom to find out which of her children had murdered the other one.

While experimenting with her hair Gretel had found a tiny egg, no bigger than the top of a pin. She showed it to Mother, who looked through her hair, pulling strands of it apart quickly, before marching over to Bruno and doing the same thing to him.

'Oh, I don't believe it,' said Mother angrily. 'I knew something like this would happen in a place like this.'

It turned out that both Gretel and Bruno had lice in their hair, and Gretel had to be treated with a special shampoo that smelled horrible and afterwards she sat in her room for hours on end, crying her eyes out.

Bruno had the shampoo as well, but then Father decided that the best thing was for him to start afresh and he got a razor and shaved all Bruno's hair off, which made Bruno cry. It didn't take long and he hated seeing all his hair float down from his head and land on the floor at his feet, but Father said it had to be done.

Afterwards Bruno looked at himself in the bathroom mirror and he felt sick. His entire head looked misshapen now that he was bald and his eyes looked too big for his face. He was almost scared of his own reflection.

'Don't worry,' Father reassured him. 'It'll grow back. It'll only take a few weeks.'

'It's the filth around here that did it,' said Mother. 'If some people could only see the effect this place is having on us all.'

When he saw himself in the mirror Bruno couldn't help but think how much like Shmuel he looked now, and he wondered whether all the people on that side of the fence had lice as well and that was why all their heads were shaved too.

When he saw his friend the next day Shmuel started to laugh at Bruno's appearance, which didn't do a lot for his dwindling self-confidence.

'I look just like you now,' said Bruno sadly, as if this was a terrible thing to admit.

'Only fatter,' admitted Shmuel.

Chapter Seventeen

Mother Gets Her Own Way

Over the course of the next few weeks Mother seemed increasingly unhappy with life at Out-With and Bruno understood perfectly well why that might be. After all, when they'd first arrived he had hated it, due to the fact that it was nothing like home and lacked such things as three best friends for life. But that had changed for him over time, mostly due to Shmuel, who had become more important to him than Karl or Daniel or Martin had ever been. But Mother didn't have a Shmuel of her own. There was no one for her to talk to, and the only person who she had been remotely friendly with – the young Lieutenant Kotler – had been transferred somewhere else.

Although he tried not to be one of those boys who spends his time listening at keyholes and down chimneys, Bruno was passing by Father's office one afternoon while Mother and Father were inside having one of their conversations. He didn't mean to eavesdrop, but they were talking quite loudly and he couldn't help but overhear.

'It's horrible,' Mother was saying. 'Just horrible. I can't stand it any more.'

'We don't have any choice,' said Father. 'This is our assignment and—'

'No, this is *your* assignment,' said Mother. '*Your* assignment, not ours. You stay if you want to.'

'And what will people think,' asked Father, 'if I permit you and the children to return to Berlin without me? They will ask questions about my commitment to the work here.'

'Work?' shouted Mother. 'You call this work?'

Bruno didn't hear much more because the voices were getting closer to the door and there was always a chance that Mother would come storming out in search of a medicinal sherry, so he ran back upstairs instead. Still, he had heard enough to know that there was a chance they might be returning to Berlin, and to his surprise he didn't know how to feel about that.

There was one part of him that remembered that he had loved his own life back there, but so many things would have changed by now. Karl and the other two best friends whose names he couldn't remember would probably have forgotten about him by now. Grandmother was dead and they almost never heard from Grandfather, who Father said had gone senile.

But on the other hand he'd grown used to life at Out-With: he didn't mind Herr Liszt, he'd become much friendlier with Maria than he ever had been back in Berlin, Gretel was still going through a phase and keeping out of his way (and she didn't seem to be quite so much of a Hopeless Case any more) and his afternoon conversations with Shmuel filled him with happiness.

Bruno didn't know how to feel and decided that whatever happened, he would accept the decision without complaint.

Nothing at all changed for a few weeks; life went on as normal. Father spent most of his time either in his office or on the other side of the fence. Mother kept very quiet during the day and was having an awful lot more of her afternoon naps, some of them not even in the afternoon but before lunch, and Bruno was worried for her health because he'd never known anyone need quite so many medicinal sherries. Gretel stayed in her room concentrating on the various maps she had pasted on the walls and consulting the newspapers for hours at a time before moving the pins around a little. (Herr Liszt was particularly pleased with her for doing this.)

And Bruno did exactly what was asked of him and caused no chaos at all and enjoyed the fact that he had one secret friend whom no one knew about.

Then one day Father summoned Bruno and Gretel

into his office and informed them of the changes that were to come.

'Sit down, children,' he said, indicating the two large leather armchairs that they were usually told not to sit in when they had occasion to visit Father's office because of their grubby mitts. Father sat down behind his desk. 'We've decided to make a few changes,' he continued, looking a little sad as he spoke. 'Tell me this: are you happy here?'

'Yes, Father, of course,' said Gretel.

'Certainly, Father,' said Bruno.

'And you don't miss Berlin at all?'

The children paused for a moment and glanced at each other, wondering which one of them was going to commit to an answer. 'Well, *I* miss it terribly,' said Gretel eventually. 'I wouldn't mind having some friends again.'

Bruno smiled, thinking about his secret.

'Friends,' said Father, nodding his head. 'Yes, I've often thought of that. It must have been lonely for you at times.'

'Very lonely,' said Gretel in a determined voice.

'And you, Bruno,' asked Father, looking at him now. 'Do you miss your friends?'

'Well, yes,' he replied, considering his answer carefully. 'But I think I'd miss people no matter where I went.' That was an indirect reference to Shmuel but he didn't want to make it any more explicit than that.

'But would you like to go back to Berlin?' asked Father. 'If the chance was there?'

'All of us?' asked Bruno.

Father gave a deep sigh and shook his head. 'Mother and Gretel and you. Back to our old house in Berlin. Would you like that?'

Bruno thought about it. 'Well, I wouldn't like it if you weren't there,' he said, because that was the truth.

'So you'd prefer to stay here with me?'

'I'd prefer all four of us to stay together,' he said, reluctantly including Gretel in that. 'Whether that was in Berlin or Out-With.'

'Oh, Bruno!' said Gretel in an exasperated voice, and he didn't know whether that was because he might be spoiling the plans for their return or because (according to her) he continued to mis-pronounce the name of their home.

'Well, for the moment I'm afraid that's going to be impossible,' said Father. 'I'm afraid that the Fury will not relieve me of my command just yet. Mother, on the other hand, thinks this would be a good time for the three of you to return home and reopen the house, and when I think about it . . .' He paused for a moment and looked out of the window to his left – the window that led off to a view of the camp on the other side of the fence. 'When I think about it, perhaps she is right. Perhaps this is not a place for children.'

'There are hundreds of children here,' said Bruno, without really thinking about his words before saying them. 'Only they're on the other side of the fence.'

A silence followed this remark, but it wasn't like a normal silence where it just happens that no one is talking. It was like a silence that was very noisy. Father and Gretel stared at him and he blinked in surprise.

'What do you mean there are hundreds of children over there?' asked Father. 'What do you know of what goes on over there?'

Bruno opened his mouth to speak but worried that he would get himself into trouble if he revealed too much. 'I can see them from my bedroom window,' he said finally. 'They're very far away of course, but it looks like there are hundreds. All wearing the striped pyjamas.'

'The striped pyjamas, yes,' said Father, nodding his head. 'And you've been watching, have you?'

'Well, I've *seen* them,' said Bruno. 'I'm not sure if that's the same thing.'

Father smiled. 'Very good, Bruno,' he said. 'And you're right, it's not quite the same thing.' He hesitated again and then nodded his head, as if he had made a final decision.

'No, she's right,' he said, speaking out loud but not looking at either Gretel or Bruno. 'She's absolutely right. You've been here long enough as it is. It's time for you to go home.'

And so the decision was made. Word was sent ahead that the house should be cleaned, the windows washed, the banister varnished, the linen pressed, the beds made, and Father announced that Mother, Gretel and Bruno would be returning to Berlin within the week.

Bruno found that he was not looking forward to this as much as he would have expected and he dreaded having to tell Shmuel the news.

Chapter Eighteen

Thinking Up the Final Adventure

The day after Father told Bruno that he would be returning to Berlin soon, Shmuel didn't arrive at the fence as usual. Nor did he show up the day after that. On the third day, when Bruno arrived there was no one sitting cross-legged on the ground and he waited for ten minutes and was about to turn back for home, extremely worried that he would have to leave Out-With without seeing his friend again, when a dot in the distance became a speck and that became a blob and that became a figure and that in turn became the boy in the striped pyjamas.

Bruno broke into a smile when he saw the figure coming towards him and he sat down on the ground, taking the piece of bread and the apple he had smuggled with him out of his pocket to give to Shmuel. But even from a distance he could see that his friend looked even more unhappy than usual, and when he got to the fence he didn't reach for the food with his usual eagerness.

'I thought you weren't coming any more,' said Bruno. 'I came yesterday and the day before that and you weren't here.'

'I'm sorry,' said Shmuel. 'Something happened.'

Bruno looked at him and narrowed his eyes, trying to guess what it might be. He wondered whether Shmuel had been told that he was going home too; after all, coincidences like that do happen, such as the fact that Bruno and Shmuel shared the same birthday.

'Well?' asked Bruno. 'What was it?'

'Papa,' said Shmuel. 'We can't find him.'

'Can't find him? That's very odd. You mean he's lost?'

'I suppose so,' said Shmuel. 'He was here on Monday and then he went on work duty with some other men and none of them have come back.'

'And hasn't he written you a letter?' asked Bruno. 'Or left a note to say when he'll be coming back?'

'No,' said Shmuel.

'How odd,' said Bruno. 'Have you looked for him?' he asked after a moment.

'Of course I have,' said Shmuel with a sigh. 'I did what you're always talking about. I did some exploration.'

'And there was no sign?'

'None.'

'Well, that's very strange,' said Bruno. 'But I think there must be a simple explanation.'

'And what's that?' asked Shmuel.

'I imagine the men were taken to work in another town and they have to stay there for a few days until the work is done. And the post isn't very good here anyway. I expect he'll turn up one day soon.'

'I hope so,' said Shmuel, who looked as if he was about to cry. 'I don't know what we're supposed to do without him.'

'I could ask Father if you wanted,' said Bruno cautiously, hoping that Shmuel wouldn't say yes.

'I don't think that would be a good idea,' said Shmuel, which, to Bruno's disappointment, was not a flat-out rejection of the offer.

'Why not?' he asked. 'Father is very knowledgeable about life on that side of the fence.'

'I don't think the soldiers like us,' said Shmuel. 'Well,' he added with something as close to a laugh as he could muster, 'I *know* they don't like us. They hate us.'

Bruno sat back in surprise. 'I'm sure they don't hate you,' he said.

'They do,' said Shmuel, leaning forward, his eyes narrowing and his lips curling up a little in anger. 'But that's all right because I hate them too. I *hate* them,' he repeated forcefully.

'You don't hate Father, do you?' asked Bruno.

Shmuel bit his lip and said nothing. He had seen Bruno's father on any number of occasions and couldn't understand how such a man could have a son who was so friendly and kind.

'Anyway,' said Bruno after a suitable pause, not wishing to discuss that topic any further, 'I have something to tell you too.'

'You do?' asked Shmuel, looking up hopefully.

'Yes. I'm going back to Berlin.'

Shmuel's mouth dropped open in surprise. 'When?' he asked, his voice catching slightly in his throat as he did so.

'Well, this is Thursday,' said Bruno. 'And we're leaving on Saturday. After lunch.'

'But for how long?' asked Shmuel.

'I think it's for ever,' said Bruno. 'Mother doesn't like it at Out-With – she says it's no place to bring up two children – so Father is staying here to work because the Fury has big things in mind for him, but the rest of us are going home.'

He said the word 'home', despite the fact that he wasn't sure where 'home' was any more.

'So I won't see you again?' asked Shmuel.

'Well, someday, yes,' said Bruno. 'You could come on a holiday to Berlin. You can't stay here for ever after all. Can you?'

Shmuel shook his head. 'I suppose not,' he said sadly. 'I won't have anyone to talk to any more when you're gone,' he added.

'No,' said Bruno. He wanted to add the words, 'I'll

miss you too, Shmuel,' to the sentence but found that he was a little embarrassed to say them. 'So tomorrow will be the last time we see each other until then,' he continued. 'We'll have to say our goodbyes then. I'll try to bring you an extra special treat.'

Shmuel nodded but couldn't find any words to express his sorrow.

'I wish we'd got to play together,' said Bruno after a long pause. 'Just once. Just to remember.'

'So do I,' said Shmuel.

'We've been talking to each other for more than a year and we never got to play once. And do you know what else?' he added. 'All this time I've been watching where you live from out of my bedroom window and I've never even seen for myself what it's like.'

'You wouldn't like it,' said Shmuel. 'Yours is much nicer,' he added.

'I'd still like to have seen it,' said Bruno.

Shmuel thought for a few moments and then reached down and put his hand under the fence and lifted it a little, to the height where a small boy, perhaps the size and shape of Bruno, could fit underneath.

'Well?' said Shmuel. 'Why don't you then?'

Bruno blinked and thought about it. 'I don't think I'd be allowed,' he said doubtfully.

'Well, you're probably not allowed to come here

and talk to me every day either,' said Shmuel. 'But you still do it, don't you?'

'But if I was caught I'd be in trouble,' said Bruno, who was sure Mother and Father would not approve.

'That's true,' said Shmuel, lowering the fence again and looking at the ground with tears in his eyes. 'I suppose I'll see you tomorrow to say goodbye then.'

Neither boy said anything for a moment. Suddenly Bruno had a brainwave.

'Unless . . .' he began, thinking about it for a moment and allowing a plan to hatch in his head. He reached a hand up to his head and felt where his hair used to be but was now just stubble that hadn't fully grown back. 'Don't you remember that you said I looked like you?' he asked Shmuel. 'Since I had my head shaved?'

'Only fatter,' conceded Shmuel.

'Well, if that's the case,' said Bruno, 'and if I had a pair of striped pyjamas too, then I could come over on a visit and no one would be any the wiser.'

Shmuel's face brightened up and he broke into a wide smile. 'Do you think so?' he asked. 'Would you do it?'

'Of course,' said Bruno. 'It would be a great adventure. Our final adventure. I could do some exploring at last.'

'And you could help me look for Papa,' said Shmuel.

'Why not?' said Bruno. 'We'll take a walk around and see whether we can find any evidence. That's always wise when you're exploring. The only problem is getting a spare pair of striped pyjamas.'

Shmuel shook his head. 'That's all right,' he said. 'There's a hut where they keep them. I can get some in my size and bring them with me. Then you can change and we can look for Papa.'

'Wonderful,' said Bruno, caught up in the enthusiasm of the moment. 'Then it's a plan.'

'We'll meet at the same time tomorrow,' said Shmuel.

'Don't be late this time,' said Bruno, standing up and dusting himself down. 'And don't forget the striped pyjamas.'

Both boys went home in high spirits that afternoon. Bruno imagined a great adventure ahead and finally an opportunity to see what was really on the other side of the fence before he went back to Berlin – not to mention getting in a little serious exploration as well – and Shmuel saw a chance to get someone to help him in the search for his papa. All in all, it seemed like a very sensible plan and a good way to say goodbye.

Chapter Nineteen

What Happened the Next Day

The next day – Friday – was another wet day. When Bruno woke in the morning he looked out of his window and was disappointed to see the rain pouring down. Had it not been for the fact that it would be the last chance for him and Shmuel to spend any time together – not to mention the fact that the adventure would be a very exciting one, especially since it involved dressing up – he would have given up on it for the day and waited until some afternoon the following week, when he didn't have anything special planned.

However, the clock was ticking and there was nothing he could do about it. And after all, it was only the morning and a lot could happen between then and the late afternoon, which was when the two boys always met. The rain would surely have stopped by then.

He watched out of the window during morning classes with Herr Liszt, but it showed no signs of slowing down then and even pounded noisily against the window. He watched during lunch from the kitchen, when it was definitely starting to ease off and there was even the hint of sunshine coming from behind a black cloud. He watched during history and geography lessons in the afternoon, when it reached its strongest force yet and threatened to knock the window in.

Fortunately it came to an end around the time that Herr Liszt was leaving, and so Bruno put on a pair of boots and his heavy raincoat, waited until the coast was clear and left the house.

His boots squelched in the mud and he started to enjoy the walk more than he ever had before. With every step he seemed to face the danger of toppling over and falling down, but he never did and managed to keep his balance, even at a particularly bad part where, when he lifted his left leg, his boot stayed implanted in the mud while his foot slipped right out of it.

He looked up at the skies, and although they were still very dark he thought the day had probably had enough rain and he would be safe enough this afternoon. Of course there would be the difficulty of explaining why he was so filthy later on when he returned home, but he could put that down to being a typical boy, which was what Mother claimed he was, and probably not get into too much trouble.

(Mother had been particularly happy over the previous few days, as each box of their belongings had been sealed and packed into a truck for despatch to Berlin.)

Shmuel was waiting for Bruno when he arrived, and for the first time ever he wasn't sitting cross-legged on the ground and staring at the dust beneath him but standing, leaning against the fence.

'Hello, Bruno,' he said when he saw his friend approaching.

'Hello, Shmuel,' said Bruno.

'I wasn't sure if we'd ever see each other again – with the rain and everything, I mean,' said Shmuel. 'I thought you might be kept indoors.'

'It was touch and go for a while,' said Bruno. 'What with the weather being so bad.'

Shmuel nodded and held out his hands to Bruno, who opened his mouth in delight. He was carrying a pair of striped pyjama bottoms, a striped pyjama top and a striped cloth cap exactly like the one he was wearing. It didn't look particularly clean but it was a disguise, and Bruno knew that good explorers always wore the right clothes.

'You still want to help me find Papa?' asked Shmuel, and Bruno nodded quickly.

'Of course,' he said, although finding Shmuel's papa was not as important in his mind as the prospect of exploring the world on the other side of the fence. 'I wouldn't let you down.'

Shmuel lifted the bottom of the fence off the ground and handed the outfit underneath to Bruno, being particularly careful not to let it touch the muddy ground below.

'Thanks,' said Bruno, scratching his stubbly head and wondering why he hadn't remembered to bring a bag to hold his own clothes in. The ground was so dirty here that they would be spoiled if he left them on the ground. He didn't have a choice really. He could either leave them here until later and accept the fact that they would be entirely caked with mud; or he could call the whole thing off and that, as any explorer of note knows, would have been out of the question.

'Well, turn round,' said Bruno, pointing at his friend as he stood there awkwardly. 'I don't want you watching me.'

Shmuel turned round and Bruno took off his overcoat and placed it as gently as possible on the ground. Then he took off his shirt and shivered for a moment in the cold air before putting on the pyjama top. As it slipped over his head he made the mistake of breathing through his nose; it did not smell very nice.

'When was this last washed?' he called out, and Shmuel turned round.

'I don't know if it's ever been washed,' said Shmuel.

'Turn round!' shouted Bruno, and Shmuel did as

he was told. Bruno looked left and right again but there was still no one to be seen, so he began the difficult task of taking off his trousers while keeping one leg and one boot on the ground at the same time. It felt very strange taking off his trousers in the open air and he couldn't imagine what anyone would think if they saw him doing it, but finally, and with a great deal of effort, he managed to complete the task.

'There,' he said. 'You can turn back now.'

Shmuel turned just as Bruno applied the finishing touch to his costume, placing the striped cloth cap on his head. Shmuel blinked and shook his head. It was quite extraordinary. If it wasn't for the fact that Bruno was nowhere near as skinny as the boys on his side of the fence, and not quite so pale either, it would have been difficult to tell them apart. It was almost (Shmuel thought) as if they were all exactly the same really.

'Do you know what this reminds me of?' asked Bruno, and Shmuel shook his head.

'What?' he asked.

'It reminds me of Grandmother,' he said. 'You remember I told you about her? The one who died?'

Shmuel nodded; he remembered because Bruno had talked about her a lot over the course of the year and had told him how fond he had been of Grandmother and how he wished he'd taken the time

203

to write more letters to her before she passed away.

'It reminds me of the plays she used to put on with Gretel and me,' Bruno said, looking away from Shmuel as he remembered those days back in Berlin, part of the very few memories now that refused to fade. 'It reminds me of how she always had the right costume for me to wear. *You wear the right outfit and you feel like the person you're pretending to be*, she always told me. I suppose that's what I'm doing, isn't it? Pretending to be a person from the other side of the fence.'

'A Jew, you mean,' said Shmuel.

'Yes,' said Bruno, shifting on his feet a little uncomfortably. 'That's right.'

Shmuel pointed at Bruno's feet and the heavy boots he had taken from the house. 'You'll have to leave them behind too,' he said.

Bruno looked appalled. 'But the mud,' he said. 'You can't expect me to go barefoot.'

'You'll be recognized otherwise,' said Shmuel. 'You don't have any choice.'

Bruno sighed but he knew that his friend was right, and he took off the boots and his socks and left them beside the pile of clothes on the ground. At first it felt horrible putting his bare feet into so much mud; they sank down to his ankles and every time he lifted a foot it felt worse. But then he started to rather enjoy it.

Shmuel reached down and lifted the base of the fence, but it only lifted to a certain height and Bruno had no choice but to roll under it, getting his striped pyjamas completely covered in mud as he did so. He laughed when he looked down at himself. He had never been so filthy in all his life and it felt wonderful.

Shmuel smiled too and the two boys stood awkwardly together for a moment, unaccustomed to being on the same side of the fence.

Bruno had an urge to give Shmuel a hug, just to let him know how much he liked him and how much he'd enjoyed talking to him over the last year.

Shmuel had an urge to give Bruno a hug too, just to thank him for all his many kindnesses, and his gifts of food, and the fact that he was going to help him find Papa.

Neither of them did hug each other though, and instead they began the walk away from the fence and towards the camp, a walk that Shmuel had done almost every day for a year now, when he had escaped the eyes of the soldiers and managed to get to that one part of Out-With that didn't seem to be guarded all the time, a place where he had been lucky enough to meet a friend like Bruno.

It didn't take long to get where they were going. Bruno opened his eyes in wonder at the things he saw. In his imagination he had thought that all the huts were full of happy families, some of whom sat outside on rocking chairs in the evening and told stories about how things were so much better when they were children and they'd had respect for their elders, not like the children nowadays. He thought that all the boys and girls who lived here would be in different groups, playing tennis or football, skipping and drawing out squares for hopscotch on the ground.

He had thought that there would be a shop in the centre, and maybe a small café like the ones he had known in Berlin; he had wondered whether there would be a fruit and vegetable stall.

As it turned out, all the things that he thought might be there – weren't.

There were no grown-ups sitting on rocking chairs on their porches.

And the children weren't playing games in groups.

And not only was there not a fruit and vegetable stall, but there wasn't a café either like there had been back in Berlin.

Instead there were crowds of people sitting together in groups, staring at the ground, looking horribly sad; they all had one thing in common: they were all terribly skinny and their eyes were sunken and they all had shaved heads, which Bruno thought must have meant there had been an outbreak of lice here too.

In one corner Bruno could see three soldiers who seemed to be in charge of a group of about twenty men. They were shouting at them, and some of the men had fallen to their knees and were remaining there with their heads in their hands.

In another corner he could see more soldiers standing around and laughing and looking down the barrels of their guns, aiming them in random directions, but not firing them.

In fact everywhere he looked, all he could see was two different types of people: either happy, laughing, shouting soldiers in their uniforms or unhappy, crying people in their striped pyjamas, most of whom seemed to be staring into space as if they were actually asleep.

'I don't think I like it here,' said Bruno after a while.

'Neither do I,' said Shmuel.

'I think I ought to go home,' said Bruno.

Shmuel stopped walking and stared at him. 'But Papa,' he said. 'You said you'd help me find him.'

Bruno thought about it. He had promised his friend that and he wasn't the sort to go back on a promise, especially when it was the last time they were going to see each other. 'All right,' he said, although he felt a lot less confident now than he had before. 'But where should we look?'

'You said we'd need to find evidence,' said

Shmuel, who was feeling upset because he thought that if Bruno didn't help him, then who would?

'Evidence, yes,' said Bruno, nodding his head. 'You're right. Let's start looking.'

So Bruno kept his word and the two boys spent an hour and a half searching the camp looking for evidence. They weren't sure exactly what they were looking for, but Bruno kept stating that a good explorer would know it when he found it.

But they didn't find anything at all that might give them a clue to Shmuel's papa's disappearance, and it started to get darker.

Bruno looked up at the sky and it looked like it might rain again. 'I'm sorry, Shmuel,' he said eventually. 'I'm sorry we didn't find any evidence.'

Shmuel nodded his head sadly. He wasn't really surprised. He hadn't really expected to. But it had been nice having his friend over to see where he lived all the same.

'I think I ought to go home now,' said Bruno. 'Will you walk back to the fence with me?'

Shmuel opened his mouth to answer, but right at that moment there was a loud whistle and ten soldiers – more than Bruno had ever seen gathered together in one place before – surrounded an area of the camp, the area in which Bruno and Shmuel were standing.

'What's happening?' whispered Bruno. 'What's going on?'

'It happens sometimes,' said Shmuel. 'They make people go on marches.'

'Marches!' said Bruno, appalled. 'I can't go on a march. I have to be home in time for dinner. It's roast beef tonight.'

'Ssh,' said Shmuel, putting a finger to his lips. 'Don't say anything or they get angry.'

Bruno frowned but was relieved that all the people in striped pyjamas from this part of the camp were gathering together now, most of them being pushed together by the soldiers, so that he and Shmuel were hidden in the centre of them and couldn't be seen. He didn't know what everyone looked so frightened about – after all, marching wasn't such a terrible thing – and he wanted to whisper to them that everything was all right, that Father was the Commandant, and if this was the kind of thing that he wanted the people to do then it must be all right.

The whistles blew again, and this time the group of people, which must have numbered about a hundred, started to march slowly together, with Bruno and Shmuel still held together in the centre. There was some sort of disturbance towards the back, where some people seemed unwilling to march, but Bruno was too small to see what happened and all he heard was loud noises, like the sound of gun-shots, but he couldn't make out what they were.

'Does the marching go on for long?' he whispered

because he was beginning to feel quite hungry now.

'I don't think so,' said Shmuel. 'I never see the people after they've gone on a march. But I wouldn't imagine it does.'

Bruno frowned. He looked up at the sky, and as he did so there was another loud sound, this time the sound of thunder overhead, and just as quickly the sky seemed to grow even darker, almost black, and rain poured down even more heavily than it had in the morning. Bruno closed his eyes for a moment and felt it wash over him. When he opened them again he wasn't so much marching as being swept along by the group of people, and all he could feel was the mud that was caked all over his body and his pyjamas clinging to his skin with all the rain and he longed to be back in his house, watching all this from a distance and not wrapped up in the centre of it.

'That's it,' he said to Shmuel. 'I'm going to catch a cold out here. I have to go home.'

But just as he said this, his feet brought him up a set of steps, and as he marched on he found there was no more rain coming down any more because they were all piling into a long room that was surprisingly warm and must have been very securely built because no rain was getting in anywhere. In fact it felt completely airtight.

'Well, that's something,' he said, glad to be out of the storm for a few minutes at least. 'I expect we'll have to wait here till it eases off and then I'll get to go home.'

Shmuel gathered himself very close to Bruno and looked up at him in fright.

'I'm sorry we didn't find your papa,' said Bruno.

'It's all right,' said Shmuel.

'And I'm sorry we didn't really get to play, but when you come to Berlin, that's what we'll do. And I'll introduce you to . . . Oh, what were their names again?' he asked himself, frustrated because they were supposed to be his three best friends for life but they had all vanished from his memory now. He couldn't remember any of their names and he couldn't picture any of their faces.

'Actually,' he said, looking down at Shmuel, 'it doesn't matter whether I do or don't. They're not my best friends any more anyway.' He looked down and did something quite out of character for him: he took hold of Shmuel's tiny hand in his and squeezed it tightly.

'You're my best friend, Shmuel,' he said. 'My best friend for life.'

Shmuel may well have opened his mouth to say something back, but Bruno never heard it because at that moment there was a loud gasp from all the marchers who had filled the room, as the door at the front was suddenly closed and a loud metallic sound rang through from the outside.

211

Bruno raised an eyebrow, unable to understand the sense of all this, but he assumed that it had something to do with keeping the rain out and stopping people from catching colds.

And then the room went very dark and somehow, despite the chaos that followed, Bruno found that he was still holding Shmuel's hand in his own and nothing in the world would have persuaded him to let it go.

Chapter Twenty

The Last Chapter

Nothing more was ever heard of Bruno after that.

Several days later, after the soldiers had searched every part of the house and gone into all the local towns and villages with pictures of the little boy, one of them discovered the pile of clothes and the pair of boots that Bruno had left near the fence. He left them there, undisturbed, and went to fetch the Commandant, who examined the area and looked to his left and looked to his right just as Bruno had done, but for the life of him he could not understand what had happened to his son. It was as if he had just vanished off the face of the earth and left his clothes behind him.

Mother did not return to Berlin quite as quickly as she had hoped. She stayed at Out-With for several months waiting for news of Bruno until one day, quite suddenly, she thought he might have made his way home alone, so she immediately returned to their old house, half expecting to see him sitting on the doorstep waiting for her.

He wasn't there, of course.

Gretel returned to Berlin with Mother and spent a lot of time alone in her room crying, not because she had thrown her dolls away and not because she had left all her maps behind at Out-With, but because she missed Bruno so much.

Father stayed at Out-With for another year after that and became very disliked by the other soldiers, whom he ordered around mercilessly. He went to sleep every night thinking about Bruno and he woke up every morning thinking about him too. One day he formed a theory about what might have occurred and he went back to the place in the fence where the pile of clothes had been found a year before.

There was nothing particularly special about this place, or different, but then he did a little exploration of his own and discovered that the base of the fence here was not properly attached to the ground as it was everywhere else and that, when lifted, it left a gap large enough for a very small person (such as a little boy) to crawl underneath. He looked into the distance then and followed it through logically, step by step by step, and when he did he found that his legs seemed to stop working right – as if they couldn't hold his body up any longer – and he ended up sitting on the ground in almost exactly the same position as Bruno had every afternoon for a year, although he didn't cross his legs beneath him.

A few months after that some other soldiers came to Out-With and Father was ordered to go with them, and he went without complaint and he was happy to do so because he didn't really mind what they did to him any more.

And that's the end of the story about Bruno and his family. Of course all this happened a long time ago and nothing like that could ever happen again.

Not in this day and age.